'Sophie...'

Bryn rose lazily ... ... breathing went in... ... business suit, he w......well, he was amazing. Tall and muscled and lean...and just plain powerful. Power oozed from every pore of his body—and from this office!

How could she ever presume to take something he wanted? Sophie wondered desperately. Like a wedding.

Trisha David is a country girl, born on a south-east Australian dairy farm. She moved on—mostly because the cows just weren't interested in her stories! Married to a 'very special doctor', Trisha writes Medical Romances® as Marion Lennox and Enchanted™ stories as Trisha David. In her other life she cares for kids, cats, dogs, chooks and goldfish, she travels, she fights her rampant garden (she's losing) and her house dust (she's lost!)—oh, and she teaches statistics and computing to undergraduates at her local university.

Recent titles by the same author:

MARRYING WILLIAM
BRIDE BY FRIDAY

BRIDE
2000

BY
TRISHA DAVID

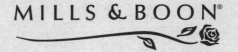

MILLS & BOON®

First published in Great Britain 1999
Harlequin Mills & Boon Limited,
Eton House, 18-24 Paradise Road, Richmond, Surrey TW9 1SR

© Trisha David 1999

ISBN 0 263 81886 1

Set in Times Roman 10½ on 11¾ pt.
02-9912-51500 C1

Printed and bound in Spain
by Litografia Rosés, S.A., Barcelona

CHAPTER ONE

'BRYN JASPER'S stolen our two thousandth wedding.'

'Has he?' Sophie Connell balanced the phone against her ear and stuck another lily in her wreath. Were there too many? She stood back, checked her arrangement critically and finally approved. Yep, this floral arrangement would do the late, lamented John Henry Jefferson proud.

'Sophie, are you listening?'

'Of course I am.' Ellie sounded overwrought, but then, Ellie always sounded overwrought. Bryn Jasper… Who on earth was Bryn Jasper?

'Sophie, you *need* to come home. Grandpa's breaking his heart, and *that man* just bulldozes everyone.'

Bryn Jasper… Oh, right! Owner of Marlin Bluff Resort and chief villain in Ellie's letters. Thanks to her sister's letters, and to society columnists, Sophie did indeed know of Bryn Jasper.

'Bryn Jasper's a businessman, Ellie. Weddings are what he does.'

'No. Weddings are what Grandpa does.'

Sophie sighed. In some ways her sister was as old-fashioned as Grandpa.

'Ellie, modern couples don't always marry in churches.'

'Some people do,' Ellie said stubbornly. 'James and I did.'

'You and James aren't exactly modern.'

'We are modern. Just because you live in New York when you should live here, it doesn't mean you know everything.' Ellie's voice was becoming hysterical. 'Sophie, you must help. It's our Millennium wedding—our two thousandth wedding and it's set...or it *was* set for next month, on the first day of January in the year 2000. Grandpa's so excited. He says he'll do it and then he'll retire, and it's the only thing that's keeping him alive.'

'Are you saying he'll turn up his toes if he doesn't get it?'

'He might.'

'Come off it, Ellie. Grandpa threatened to turn up his toes if I came to New York, and that was six years ago.'

'Well, he means it now,' her sister retorted. 'If Bryn Jasper keeps stealing our brides I don't know how Grandpa can bear it, and Grandpa's so honourable! He won't even tell me who it is that's cancelled so I can go and see them. Sophie, it's time you came home. I can't take on Bryn Jasper by myself.'

'You want me to come home and take on your villain?'

'Yes, I do. You owe it to us, Sophie.'

Sophie sighed and hardened her heart. She was accustomed to her sister's emotional blackmail—but then she paused and looked out at the sleet-covered street in front of her elegant New York florist shop. The pavement was wind-blasted and freezing, a garbage strike was running into a third week and the streets were filthy.

Sophie had done six funerals in the last two weeks, while Rick had done every wedding. Marlin Bluff, on the other hand, where Ellie was ringing from...

It would be the start of the rainy season in Northern Queensland. Her sister would be looking out of the window to gardens that were lush and tropical and soaking. It would be dripping wet, the same as here, but lovely wet. The rainforest would be growing while Ellie watched. There would be tree frogs croaking, the sun would be coming out between rain showers and steaming everything in sight…and a sudden wave of homesickness hit Sophie with such fierceness that her decision was easy.

Rick could take over the funerals for a month or so. He could cope with the sleet and the garbage—and it'd serve him right for taking all the weddings. 'Okay, Ellie,' she told the telephone, and listened to the stunned silence with a mischievous grin. 'I'll come home and steal your two thousandth wedding back from Bryn Jasper.'

'You're kidding.'

'Nope.' Sophie suddenly had a vision of a millennium wedding as it could be, set in the tiny chapel overlooking the sea at Marlin Bluff. Grandpa would be wearing his gorgeous crimson robes and the chapel would be crammed with every flower she could lay her hands on—flame flowers, frangipani, calla lilies and spinning gum.

It would be the first marriage of the Millennium, and it would be a wedding to remember for the next thousand years…if she could only steal one bride back from Bryn Jasper.

Maybe she could and maybe she couldn't, but it might be fun to try. Could she pip the great Bryn Jasper at the post? It might be just the sort of challenge she was craving.

'Nope,' she said again. 'I kid you not. Bring on your villains, Ellie, love. Let's put on a Millennium wedding to die for. Bryn Jasper, here I come.'

CHAPTER TWO

THE track was normally deserted or he'd never have let them go. No one used this track, and especially no one used this track in the middle of a tropical rainstorm. Bryn stood stunned for all of two seconds before launching himself forward to find out who was under his two dogs.

It was a girl. No, it was a woman, and she was lying flat on her back in thick mud. Her white linen dress was a muddy mess, her short black curls were soaking and plastered around her lovely face, and the wide grey eyes that looked up at him over steaming dog were…

They were laughing!

'Get them off! Oh, you brutes…' Sophie shoved the two Great Danes away from her face and tried to sit up. The dogs kept right on licking. They placed their big, soft paws onto Sophie's shoulders—a dog on each side—and she collapsed into helpless laughter under their vast, licking tongues.

'Marty. Goggle. Off!' Bryn's shock eased enough to let him move. He grabbed a collar apiece, and tried to haul his dogs away. He didn't have much luck. The dogs were slippery and strong, and wildly excited with their find.

Their 'find' was also in shock. One minute Sophie had been walking along the track she'd used for years to walk home from school; the next she was lying flat on her back with the hounds from hell licking her into the mud. And now…in between dog licks she was staring up at the most stunning male torso she'd ever seen.

Bryn had brought his dogs out for a serious run. It was

hot and wet, so he'd dressed accordingly, wearing brief shorts and running shoes—and nothing else.

Sophie stared up through the tangle of dogs and she knew who this was. She'd seen Bryn's picture in society magazines and she would have recognised his piercing, hawk-like eyes anywhere. The rest, though…

Bryn had long legs; they were built like oak, and they led to shorts…

Forget the shorts. They were far too brief for her comfort, so she blinked, swallowed, and forced her eyes higher. He had a chest like a barrel—a long, lean barrel—the sort made from aged oak with vast steel struts for ribs…

Yeah? She was fantasising here. She was lying in the mud in the pouring rain with two dogs trying to lick her senseless and she was having extremely silly thoughts about a man who was practically standing on top of her.

But those eyes… Dear heaven, those eyes! They were deeply set in a strongly boned face, they were dark brown to match his tan, and they crinkled at the edges as he looked down at her with concern. There were rivulets of water running down Bryn's forehead, making his jet-black hair cling in wet curling strands—but mostly all she saw was his eyes. A girl could drown in those eyes…

She had to say something. Sophie opened her mouth as Bryn finally succeeded in hauling his dogs backward, and she gave it her best shot.

'Hi!'

As greetings went, it was pathetic, and it sounded whimperish—mostly because she had a mouthful of mud—but it made Bryn's eyes snap together in concern. Hell, she wasn't hurt…

'Are you okay?'

'Oh, yeah, I'm fine. Never better. Mud massages are great for a person's health, didn't you know?' She stag-

gered to her feet and managed a grin. 'Do I have the pleasure of addressing Bryn Jasper?'

That took him aback. Bryn stood and dripped rainwater,
with his dogs only barely under control, and he felt more
off balance than he'd ever felt in his life.

'Yes,' he managed. 'Who the…?'

'Who the hell am I?' Sophie smiled, and her smile was
dazzling, mud and all. 'I'm Sophie Connell, but don't expect me to shake hands, because your prime task, Mr
Jasper—your only task, in fact—is to hang onto those dogs.
What did you call them?'

'Marty and Goggle. But…'

'Why?'

Bryn floundered. He'd dated some of the loveliest
women in the world, he had a staff of hundreds but, for the
first time in as long as he could remember, he was totally
out of his depth.

'I beg your pardon?'

'Why are they called Marty and Goggle? I would have
thought something like Dope and Stupid might be more
appropriate. Or Thug One and Thug Two.'

Bryn smiled then. It was the first time Sophie had seen
him smile, and the erotic thoughts she'd had when she'd
first seen him grew more erotic by the minute. The tabloids
called him one of the world's most eligible bachelors and
she could see why!

'They're named after my mother's goldfish.'

'Yeah?' Most women would have stared and demanded
a reason, but Sophie did no such thing. She searched around
until she found her bags in the mud, then she grasped her
suitcases and hitched them up by her side—businesslike
and ready to move on. 'I can see that.'

'You can see it?'

'Brains of...' she said simply. 'Their IQs should just about match. Yep, I can see your mother's point of view.'

'As a matter of fact,' Bryn said carefully, 'I renamed the dogs to placate her when they ate them.'

'Gee, I bet that helped.' Sophie hoisted the strap of her bag over her shoulder and took a determined step forward. 'If they'd eaten me, would you have renamed them Sophie One and Sophie Two? How many names have they had, Mr Jasper?' Then, before he could reply, she shook her head, dismissing him nicely. 'Well, I can't say it was nice meeting you, but it's been interesting. Goodbye.'

'Where are you going?' Bryn asked faintly. There was nothing along this track except the chapel and the old vicar's residence, and her baggage looked really heavy.

'I'm going to my grandpa's. He's the vicar of St Marks.'

'Your grandfather is the vicar of St Marks?'

'Very good,' she said, approving. 'A great body and intelligence as well, plus two wonderful, superbly trained, goldfish-eating dogs. Your mother must be the proudest lady! Now, if you'll excuse me...' And she waited with obvious patience for him to stand aside.

'You're walking to your grandfather's?' He was starting to sound fatuous here, and it made Sophie grin. She had him nicely off balance and it wouldn't hurt to leave him that way.

'Well, that was the intention, but I could swim if this rain gets much heavier.'

But Bryn had a whole heap of questions crowding in and he wanted answers. He wasn't being put aside with sarcasm.

'Where did you spring from?'

'From under a mushroom?' Sophie sighed, and kept right on smiling her 'nice lady humouring the village imbecile' smile. 'Sorry, I was joking. Even this rainforest doesn't grow mushrooms that big. I've come from New York.'

'New York!'

'That's in the United States of America,' Sophie added kindly—and that was the end. Bryn's control broke and he choked on laughter as his eyes warmed with admiration. This lady was enchanting!

'Let me help. I'll carry your…' He reached forward for her cases—and he was so far off balance that he released his dogs to do it. Mistake! She staggered back under their combined assault; Bryn launched himself forward to grab her shoulders over the dogs, then gripped to stop her falling. The dogs yelped with joy, Sophie choked on laughter, and Bryn swore and gripped tighter.

'Get lost, you stupid mutts. I'll have you turned into horsemeat. Of all the stupid…'

He shoved them sideways—and suddenly there were no dogs between them. Bryn's bare chest was pressed against Sophie's breasts, her breath was on his face and her wide, luminous eyes were laughing right up into his as he held her tight.

He could hardly breathe. She was the most gorgeous…

'Excuse me, but would you mind letting me go?' Sophie pulled herself back to arm's length, so her breasts weren't crushed against his chest. Stupidly, she didn't like doing it—there was a tiny part of her that had wanted to stay right where she was—and she didn't pull right out of his arms. Still he held her, not letting any dog between them.

She didn't protest further, but eyed the dogs warily from the safety of his hold. 'No, I'm not trying to escape, boys,' she told them. 'If necessary I'll stand here until you go home for dinner—just please don't think I'm it.'

'Sophie, I'm sorry…'

'Mr Jasper, can we just think of a way where I can quietly pick up my gear and keep walking?' she begged. 'It's a tough task, I know, but I'm a lady with simple needs.'

'Hell!'

'No, don't swear. That doesn't work either. Just think.'

How on earth could he think when he was looking at her? The mud and the rain made Sophie's dress almost transparent. The fabric was clinging to every lovely line of her body, and her breasts were two soft, pliant mounds, tipped with...

Get a hold on yourself, Bryn told himself grimly. Think.

What should he do here? Sure, he could drag his dogs off and leave, but he badly didn't want to do that. He wanted to help her with her baggage, but mainly he wanted to stay right where he was, holding her in his arms.

He closed his eyes—it was the only way thought was possible and when he opened them he had the answer. He shoved a hand down to his belt, to the pouch holding his phone. While Sophie watched, still staying less than an arm's length away, he shoved it into action and barked an order. Luckily the mud hadn't drowned it.

'Joe? Where are you? Do we have a man on the northern boundary? I'm on the chapel track and I need someone to fetch the dogs. You're close? Great. Fast, Joe, it's urgent.'

He snapped the phone back in its pouch and turned back to Sophie. That was a mistake. Sophie was staring up at him in blatant admiration, and his heart suddenly started beating way too fast for someone who'd barely started his daily exercise.

'Hey, I wish I had a Joe,' she said softly, her voice lilting with laughter. 'I'd get a dog if I had a Joe.' She smiled, her lovely eyes twinkling. 'I might even get myself a husband and a couple of kids. I can imagine it now. "Joe, cook a casserole, walk the kids and make sure hubby doesn't watch too much golf on television."' With a Joe included, marriage looks more appealing than it ever has before.'

Bryn managed a grin in return. They were ankle-deep in mud, the dogs were panting behind them ready to lunge at a moment's notice, and they must look totally ridiculous, but all of a sudden Bryn didn't care. He wanted to know more about this woman, and he wanted to know *now*.

'I doubt if Joe would play housemaid in a marriage. He's more interested in the husband role.' He quirked an eyebrow. 'But by that I take it that you're not married?' It was crazy to be exchanging social niceties in this position, but his need to know was urgent.

'No way.' Sophie smiled. 'Marriage doesn't fit my image.' She looked ruefully down at herself. 'If I still have an image somewhere under this mess. And you?'

Bryn was accustomed to asking questions—not fielding them. Her question took him aback.

'No. I'm not married.'

'Because it doesn't suit your image?'

'I don't have time for a wife and children,' he said shortly.

'Because you're too busy with your dogs,' she finished kindly. 'I can see that. You must spend half of every day in training, they're so well behaved.'

'Sophie…'

'Yes?' She gave him her very sweetest smile.

'If you give me a hard time, then I'll let my dogs at you again,' Bryn warned, and Sophie held up her hands in mock horror.

'No. Oh, no, Mr Jasper, sir. Anything but that!' And then she took a deep breath and did something she'd been dying to do ever since she'd climbed from the bus and felt rain on her face. It was something she and Ellie had done every wet day they could, and home wasn't home until she'd done it.

She pulled back, did a surreptitious check behind her to make sure she was heading for a soft landing, and fell full-length back into the mud, sending up a spray of black water as she fell.

It was the very best way to make a mud angel…

Bryn stared. What the…? What on earth was this? This girl-woman. This *nut*!

But Sophie's grey eyes were dancing up at him from where she was lying in the mud, and he could no more resist their appeal than he could fly. He found himself laughing, a full throated, rumbling laugh that sounded out through the rain forest. Of all the ridiculous, crazy…

And that was how Joe the groundsman found them two seconds later when he rounded the last bend in the track. His employer was bent double with laughter and a woman Joe faintly recognised was lying full length in the mud. The dogs were looking on with absolute bemusement.

'Excuse me, sir…'

He said it twice before it reached them, and from where she lay Sophie's smile widened in recognition. The groundsman was unmistakable, a man about her age with a jagged scar slashing his face from his forehead to collar. Joe… She lay in the mud and sighed with pleasure. She'd made a mud angel and Joe was here. Now she knew she was truly home.

'You wanted me, sir?' Joe asked, before Bryn found his voice. He looked doubtfully down at Sophie, trying to figure things out. 'I mean…are you in trouble?'

'Oh, he's in trouble,' Sophie said direfully, trying to straighten her mud-splattered face. She was still lying flat on her back and the mud felt just lovely underneath her. 'He was threatening me. Remember how you saw me, Joe?

This is me collapsed in horror. I could develop real emotional trauma from this.' Her twinkling eyes turned thoughtful. 'Hey, I'll bet I could sue the pants off you, Bryn Jasper.'

Joe chuckled, his eyes growing warm as he, in turn, recognised her. 'Well, well, it's Sophie—and threatening mayhem already. Excuse me, Sophie, but Mr Jasper doesn't appear to have much in the way of pants *on* right now. I wouldn't want to see him with less.'

The groundsman limped across and put down a hand to help her rise. 'Sophie, you're a nut. You always have been and you always will be, and it's great to see you. Ellie told me you were coming. Your grandpa will be as pleased as punch to have you home.'

'Even like this?' Sophie chuckled and gave him a solid hug, mud and all. 'Hey, Joe, I didn't know you were working for the great Bryn Jasper. How's your mum?'

'Mum's fine, and she'll be tickled pink to see you.'

'Excuse me,' Bryn said carefully, staring from one to the other. 'Sophie, I was going to introduce you to Joe, my head groundsman, but… Joe, I gather you already know this…'

'This lovely young lady?' Sophie supplied sweetly. 'Was that what you were going to say, Mr Jasper?'

'Yeah. Right.'

'Lunatic, more like,' Joe amended. He grinned at his employer. 'Of course I know Sophie. We shared our first cigarette—and our last—behind the shelter sheds at the local school, and I'll never forget her mud angels.' He stared down at the imprint Sophie had left squelched in the mud across the track, and his eyes crinkled in remembrance. 'She and Ellie made mud angels all over the place. They tried to make as many as they could right at the end of the wet, so all through the dry you'd round a bend in the track and there'd be an imprint of the two of them. Sophie lived here with her grandpa for years before she took off to America to make her fortune.' He smiled at Sophie. 'And Ellie tells me you've done it. She's *so* proud!'

'I haven't made a fortune…'

'Ellie showed Mum a glossy magazine—some publication or other Mum says is just the most fashionable thing—and it had your florist shop in New York written up as a feature. The floral arrangements were amazing.' He turned to Bryn. 'Sophie was always a dab hand with flowers, but what she's done now… Ellie says she's won international awards.'

'Joe, my head will swell if you keep going on like this,' Sophie told him. She was aware of Bryn's eyes on her, and was suddenly acutely conscious that her dress was clinging far too close. She took a deep breath and tried grabbing her suitcase again. 'If you gentlemen will excuse me, can you control these hounds from hell while I go on to Grandpa's?'

'I'll walk Miss Connell home,' Bryn said brusquely. 'Joe, if you'll take the dogs…'

'How about if Joe walks me home and you take your own dogs?' Sophie suggested, slightly breathlessly. 'Joe and I being old friends and all.'

'Nope.'

'No.'

Joe and Bryn spoke as one, and Joe eyed his employer speculatively and then smiled.

'You take Miss Sophie home,' he told Bryn kindly. 'Seems to me, I'm her old friend and maybe this is a chance for her to make a new one.' His grin broadened. 'If I'm not mistaken, Sophie could be a really interesting friend for you to know. Here, Marty. Here, Goggle.' Joe clicked his fingers—and the Great Danes fell obediently behind him,

for all the world like two well-trained dogs. Then he turned
on his heels and limped away, leaving them to each other.

Silence.

To stand in pouring rain in the mud when the two dogs
were there seemed funny. To stand there now seemed just
silly, and all at once Sophie felt silly. Making mud angels
had been something she'd loved doing since she was knee-
high to a grasshopper. She and Ellie had turned mud-
floundering into an art form—almost an Olympic sport—
but she was now twenty-eight—not six years old—and
she'd done it in front of Bryn Jasper! The man would think
she was a total twit.

She stared up at him, confused. Bryn was still too naked,
and too close, and altogether too darned male for comfort.

'Are you really going to sue the pants off me?' he asked
mildly, and she stared down at his pants and blushed bright
crimson.

'Heck, no,' she managed. 'Not when Joe's told me I
shouldn't.'

'Joe really is an old friend?'

'He is.' Sophie tilted her chin and looked at Bryn, her
face creasing into a frown of concentration. 'But…I don't
understand. With Joe's limp… After the accident he lost so
much school that he dropped two grades and ended up in
my year. That's how we became friends. I knew he wanted
to be a gardener, but his mother said he'd never be able to
work outdoors.'

'He's working now.'

'As your head groundsman?'

'That's right. It's mostly a supervisory role, and not too
physically demanding. The man knows his plants and he's
the best foreman I've ever had. He can handle it.'

Silence.

'Do you want to go on?' Bryn asked at last, but Sophie shook her head, still concentrating.

'Wait. I'm trying to figure this out.' She brushed the rain from her eyes. 'Last time Joe's mum wrote to me, she told me he was classed as unemployable by Social Welfare unless he does desk work,' Sophie said slowly. 'If he has an accident at work, his employer may end up paying out. Even though he's been breaking his heart to do this sort of work, and he's done every course known to man, his mum said no one would put him on.'

There was no comment, and Sophie looked sideways at Bryn as she thought it through. Ellie had described this man as a ruthless businessman, but that didn't fit with him employing Joe. He'd taken her baggage, and they took a few steps along the track before she spoke again.

'But you did take him on?' she asked.

Still no comment.

'You're supposed to be a businessman who lets nothing stand in your way of a profit,' Sophie probed. 'I don't understand.'

'Meaning you wouldn't put Joe on in your florist shop?'

'Hey, there's me and Rick and a million flowers in my florist shop,' Sophie told him. 'Anyone else and we'd be hanging out the windows.'

'You know what I mean.'

'Meaning I couldn't afford the risk of employing Joe? You might be right,' she admitted. 'But I still don't understand…'

'Joe gives good value for money. Now let's leave it.' Bryn strode on so fast that Sophie had to struggle to keep up. Her feet squelched in the mud and the rain was getting stronger by the minute. 'Miss Connell, did it ever occur to you that there are taxi drivers whose only purpose in life is to take people in air-conditioned comfort from the airport to their homes? And there's a bituminised road from the south.'

'Gee, why didn't I think of that?' she said in admiration, and Bryn sighed.

'Don't tell me. You couldn't afford the fare—just like you couldn't afford to employ Joe.'

'That must be it.'

'If you've a florist shop in New York...'

'With Rick. He keeps me in style, but without him I'm reduced to penury,' she said cheerfully. 'What's the problem, Mr Jasper? Baggage too heavy? I didn't have any problem carrying it. Here, let me help.'

But Bryn jerked her suitcases away, and his look was one of concentration, as if trying to figure out just what made her tick.

'You're home for a while?' he demanded.

'Yep.'

'Just to visit your grandfather?'

'And Ellie and James and Pete and Lily and Susan and Matilda and...'

'Whoa... Who are...? No, don't tell me. Ellie's your sister. James will be Ellie's husband. I've met him. They live in Port Douglas but they spend heaps of time here. Pete and Susan and Lily and Matilda...are they their kids?'

'Not quite.' Sophie chuckled contentedly. It felt good to be home, to be walking along this familiar track, the mud squelching out between her toes in the open sandals just like it used to do—and it felt good to be walking side by side with this man... 'Pete and Susan are Ellie's kids. Lily and Matilda are Labradors.'

'Fat black ones. I know them.' He grinned. 'At least, Marty and Goggle have met them.'

'Marty and Goggle haven't eaten them?' Sophie demanded, her voice laced with misgiving, and Bryn's grin broadened.

'Miss Connell, I defy anyone to eat those Labradors. If they were beef cattle they'd keep a family of twelve in meat for a year. Of all the fat, useless…'

'There's no reason to be rude.' She put her nose in the air and sniffed. 'Lily was my dog before I left home and I love her dearly. It's not her fault she's addicted to licorice allsorts.'

'And you think my dogs are untrained!'

'Mr Jasper, I can very well walk home by myself,' she said with dignity. 'Hand over my baggage. I won't allow nasturtiums to be cast at my darling Lily.'

'You'd defend her to the death?'

'If I must.' Sophie grabbed a suitcase, but it wasn't released. She stood still, her hand over Bryn's on her suitcase handle, and she started feeling decidedly odd. It was the feel of his hand on hers. There was warmth flooding through her from her hand—warmth and something else. It was something she didn't understand, and it was making her desperately want to move closer…

She did no such thing. Instead, Sophie pulled her baggage away with more desperation than dignity, and tried for a formal farewell.

'Mr Jasper, please don't come further. I…I would like to…to end my walk alone. Thank you for rescuing me from Marty and Goggle, but now…'

Bryn was having none of it. He leaned forward and took her suitcase firmly back into his grasp, brooking no argument, and she had a choice of an uneven tug of war, in which there could only be one winner, or accepting that he carry the dratted thing.

She released the suitcase, but she glowered.

'That's better,' Bryn approved. 'Now just squelch along

beside me like a good girl, and we'll forget about trading insults for a minute.'

'Why?' Sophie's glower deepened. 'I like trading insults. With you it seems to come naturally.'

'Maybe, but you shouldn't trade insults with a potential employer,' Bryn said kindly. 'Miss Connell, shut up for a minute. I'm about to offer you a job.'

CHAPTER THREE

A JOB...

Sophie's mind went into overdrive as Bryn outlined his proposition, and why he suddenly needed a florist. 'I need help,' he told her. 'Unfortunately, my florist's developed a passion for one of my clerks.'

'Unfortunately?'

'Yes. Unfortunately. Brian was engaged to one of the housemaids when Wendy showed an interest.' Bryn sighed. 'In the end I had to dismiss her. Brian left too, leaving me with no clerk, no florist and a housemaid suffering a broken heart.'

'It's a bit ruthless to sack people for having an affair,' Sophie said cautiously, and he nodded.

'Yep. Normally I don't mind the odd affair. It keeps life interesting. It was only when Wendy threw crayfish brûlée over Maureen in the middle of a frantic time in our top restaurant—and missed and hit a patron—that I thought enough was enough.'

She choked. 'Really?'

He spread his hands. 'There are some things even the most tolerant employers can't put up with. So now I'm in dire trouble.'

'I can't imagine a resort like yours having trouble finding staff.'

'House staff, maybe, but florists... Wendy was one of the best, and I need someone with her talent.'

'So you'd take me on, sight unseen? Sight of my work, I mean,' Sophie said hurriedly as Bryn's smile widened.

Her clinging dress meant there was little that he couldn't see.

'I don't have much choice,' Bryn admitted, his smile fading. 'Joe sings your praises, if you make a living arranging flowers in New York then you must be good, and I'm operating now with a florist's assistant. I've tried everywhere to find a replacement, but with the Millennium coming up no one's free. Louise—the assistant—is only just competent. My last two brides have been disappointed.'

'Oh, dear.'

He smiled again, with his wonderful smile that had the power to hold her in thrall—and to talk her into doing something she didn't want to do.

'I know it sounds minor, but I guarantee my brides the best of everything. If they can have better flowers if they marry in Cairns or Sydney—or even in New York—then I'm not doing my job.'

'But…' Sophie chewed her bottom lip and drank some rainwater, buying herself time. 'Mr Jasper, I'm here on holiday.'

'I'm not offering you a full-time job,' he told her, as they trudged on through the rain. 'But if you'll keep one magnificent floral arrangement fresh in the foyer, give instructions to Louise as to what she should put on the tables and alcoves, and do the weddings…'

'How many weddings?' she asked cautiously.

'I have three a week booked through until the end of the year. That's in four weeks. Then we have one booked on the first of January, and I intend that to be our major, all-stops-pulled-out wedding of the century. It's the first wedding of the new Millennium and I've arranged worldwide coverage. It has to be the best, and that's one of the reasons I'm so worried about having a decent florist. What do you say?'

What did she say? She stared down at her muddy toes and tried to think of something—anything. She was here on holiday and she didn't want to work, but…three weddings a week…

If there was one thing Sophie loved above all else it was arranging wedding flowers, and to do them here, with no expense spared and with all this tropical foliage to work with… It would be wonderful. Magic!

There was a problem. The Millennium wedding was the wedding she hoped to steal back for Grandpa, she reminded herself, but…what better way to steal back a wedding than to do it from the inside? Interview the bride about her flowers and sow a few doubts. *Why aren't you marrying in the chapel? I could do the flowers for you for free, and, really, chapel weddings are so much more romantic—oh, and have you seen my grandfather in his crimson robes?*

It reeked of…challenge?

Sophie looked up at Bryn and her eyes twinkled in a way he found entirely disconcerting. He was a businessman, after all, she decided. All was fair in love and war—and business!

'Okay, Mr Jasper,' she said softly. 'You're on. You have yourself a florist. I'm charging New York rates, though.'

'Accepted. I reserve the right to reconsider after I see your first wedding, but if your work's up to standard I have no problem paying the going rate.'

'It will be up to standard,' Sophie promised. 'Bring on your weddings, Mr Jasper. I think I'm about to have some fun.'

As a surprise homecoming, it took some beating. Sophie had told her grandfather she'd be home on Saturday, but a last-minute cancellation had freed her to catch a plane a day early, so now she walked in, unexpected, coated with mud and with a near naked Bryn Jasper beside her.

Ellie was in the kitchen with the children, Grandpa was at the table with a grandchild on each knee and the dogs were at his feet. All of them stared in amazement as Sophie entered—and then they stared at Bryn.

'I've brought your granddaughter home,' Bryn said, and smiled as if he was doing everyone a huge favour. There was no comment on the state he'd produced her in!

'Hi,' Sophie said, and she still sounded pathetic.

John Connell was the first to recover. He set the children on their feet and caught his sodden granddaughter in a bear hug, then, looking over her dripping curls, his welcome enveloped Bryn.

'We'd heard she was coming home by aeroplane but…brought her home by sea, then, did you, boy?'

That broke the ice. Peter and Susan, five and three years old, started whooping, the Labradors started barking, Ellie smiled through her shock, and somehow Bryn managed to make it back to the door.

'I'll see you tomorrow, Sophie.' He smiled again, that all-enveloping smile that made her insides turn somersaults. 'Nine a.m. at the resort? No…' He held up a hand as John released Sophie. 'Don't see me out. You've got a handful there, sir.' His grin widened as he turned and left, leaving Ellie staring after him in open-mouthed astonishment.

'Sophie, what on earth…?'

Sophie pulled away from Grandpa and hauled her sister into her arms. 'Hey, Ellie, aren't you pleased to see me? You seem more interested in Bryn than in your sister.'

'No. Yes.' Ellie pulled back and held Sophie at arm's length. 'Sophie, would you mind telling me what is going on?'

'I'm home.' Sophie grabbed Ellie and swung her around in a circle. 'What could be more important than that?'

'I don't know,' Ellie said cautiously, trying not to be swung. 'Maybe nothing. But...'

'But what?'

'That *was* Bryn Jasper with you just now?'

'It sure was.' Sophie moved on to Peter and Susan and swung them high, one child in each arm. 'Good grief! You guys have grown half a head apiece! You'll be taller than me soon.'

'Sophie...'

'And Lily and Matilda...' Sophie fell to her knees, hugging the dogs close. 'You remember me. Of course you remember me.' Then, as the dogs' licking grew frantic, she paused and drew back. 'Hey, that's not me you're greeting. That's a dog-smells-dog greeting. Just because I have the smell of Marty and Goggle all over me...'

'Marty and Goggle?' Ellie said faintly.

'Bryn's dogs.'

'Bryn's dogs...' Ellie placed her hands on her hips and glared. 'Sophie Connell, if you don't tell me what's going on I'll scream. Where did you meet Bryn Jasper? Why are you filthy, and why are you meeting him tomorrow? And are you aware that the man had practically nothing on?' Her voice rose to practically a squeak. 'Sophie!'

'Now I know I'm home,' Sophie said warmly, hauling her dogs back in close. 'Dogs in my arms, kids in the kitchen and Ellie having hysterics. Oh, Grandpa, it feels good to be back.'

'It's good to have you back,' John said calmly. 'But, Sophie, I think you'd best tell your sister what's happening before she carries out her threat.' He eyed his older grand-daughter with caution. Ellie was thirty years old, but she'd been known to carry out threats before.

'Hey, Grandpa, there's nothing to it.' Sophie smiled up at all her family. 'Bryn's dogs knocked me over in the mud, he's offered me a job as a florist, and now I intend to take back our wedding. That's what I came home to do, and my plan is progressing nicely.'

'Sophie,' Ellie said faintly.

'I can't see anything wrong with that,' Sophie said defensively. 'If the world's greatest spies can infiltrate, sabotage and win, I don't see why I can't. Do you?'

It had been easy to sound confident when Sophie was surrounded by her family, but at nine the next morning she wasn't so sure. Marlin Bluff Resort was fabulous. Sophie walked up the palm-lined driveway and had to practically shut her jaw by hand.

Bryn's hotel was built of gleaming white stone, low and long and vast, set against the backdrop of the turquoise water of the Great Barrier Reef. A warm wind sighed through the palms and gentle waves washed in and out in dreamy rhythm on the beach beyond. The long, open-planned building practically beckoned you inside. It was built so that in fine weather the walls could be folded right back, disappearing so the place was open to the mountains on one side and the sea on the other. The foyer was an acre wide, and furnished in magnificent, understated luxury…

Sophie crossed the entrance bridge, trod up the Italian tiled steps, waved aside a doorman who came forward to welcome her and made her way through clusters of vast settees and chairs and floral arrangements.

There were flowers everywhere. No wonder Bryn needed a florist. Sophie eyed them with delight as she made her way to reception. The flowers themselves were magnificent, but her fingers were already itching to rearrange.

What a place! Wealth screamed from everywhere.

Outside was the swimming pool—and what a swimming pool! It surrounded the entire hotel. It must cover acres, and was built with natural sand sweeping up to artificial beaches, so the eye wasn't sure where pool ended and beach began. A few swimmers were doing lazy laps of its width, and a uniformed youth was laying vast white towels on loungers that screamed to be laid on…

How could one work in a place like this? Sophie thought. One wallowed in a place like this—and Bryn owned it! And Sophie was here to take something Bryn wanted. How could she ever convince a couple to have their wedding any place other than here?

Grandpa's chapel wasn't opulent and luxurious; it was simple and plain, but its very simplicity was lovely. It overlooked the sea, with worn wooden floors, pews polished with age and a stained glass window at the altar where the sun glinted in from the sea.

It could compete. It could! She took a deep breath, smoothed down her chic little skirt—she'd worn a neat linen suit for what she figured was really a job interview—and made her way to reception.

'James Bond would do this,' she muttered. 'Just because he's male doesn't mean he's the only one who can infiltrate and win. Just call me Jane Bond and here I go.'

'I'm Jane… I mean, I'm Sophie Connell,' she said to the receptionist, and had to suppress a grin at what her brain was doing to her. 'Mr Jasper is expecting me.'

'Miss Connell…' The girl gave Sophie her very brightest smile, curiosity evident. 'Mr Jasper's told me all about you. Come right this way.' She led the way to the right, with Sophie wondering uneasily just what had been said about her. Mad lady who lies in mud?

Bryn's office was no less imposing than the rest of the place. The receptionist knocked on double oak doors, swung the door wide for her to pass and it was all she could do not to gasp. Instead, she managed to school her face and pretend it was an everyday occurrence to walk into offices as big as a small golf course. Bryn's desk was the size of a putting green, and French windows looked out over the sea all the way to Hawaii…

'Sophie…'

Bryn rose lazily from behind his desk and her breathing went into gasp mode all over again. Yesterday he'd been near naked and gorgeous. Fully dressed now, in a sleek Italian business suit, he was…well, he was amazing. Tall and muscled and lean…and just plain powerful. Power oozed from every pore of his body—and from this office!

How could she ever presume to take something he wanted? Sophie wondered desperately. Like a wedding.

'Bryn,' she managed. She was doing this man a favour, she reminded herself sharply as she spoke. She didn't need this man's job and she didn't need his money. She just wanted his wedding.

'Where are Marty and Goggle?' she asked as he came around the desk to take her hand. Hey, it was just a handshake, after all. There was no reason for her breathing to falter as his fingers touched hers. 'I…I thought of bringing a tranquilliser gun, just in case.'

'They're out with Joe.' Bryn had the grace to look abashed. 'They get bored with me.'

'I'll bet they do—and it's so bad for business to have them eating your guests.' She grinned and eyed Bryn from head to toe, wishing he'd release her hand. It was doing strange things to her insides. 'Goodness! You scrub up well.'

Bryn's dark eyebrows quirked upward. Clearly he was unaccustomed to such familiarity, but laughter sprang into his eyes.

'I could say the same for you, Miss Connell,' he told her, his eyes warmly approving. 'Welcome to Marlin Bluff.' The hand holding hers was strong and warm, and Sophie's colour was mounting, whether she willed it or not.

'There's no need to welcome me to Marlin Bluff,' she managed, her smile slipping as her hand was finally released. 'I've been here since yesterday.'

'I meant welcome to Marlin Bluff Resort.'

That took her aback. 'You refer to this place as Marlin Bluff, without adding "Resort" to the title?'

'Well, yes.' Bryn's smile stayed in place. 'There's not a lot here *but* the resort.'

'There's people who've lived here a lot longer than you and had never dreamed of Marlin Bluff Resort until you came,' Sophie retorted.

'"People" meaning you?'

'Yes.' Sophie's annoyance was growing. 'Marlin Bluff was a viable community before your resort was built.'

'No, it wasn't,' he said gently, watching her face. 'Marlin Bluff was dying and you have to admit it. Even your grandfather's chapel is closing.'

'Because you've taken all his weddings.'

'Hey, that's a bit unfair.' Bryn stood back and eyed Sophie with a frown. 'A chapel has more than just weddings—but your grandfather's parishioners have moved on, haven't they, Sophie?' he said softly, not without sympathy. 'Port Douglas has grown so much it provides everything Marlin Bluff used to provide—and more. That all happened before I opened this resort. I'm not a big, bad developer buying your grandfather's church and throwing him out. The church is closing, regardless. There's no need to blame me for it.'

'But…'

'But what?'

Sophie sighed and tried to smile. 'I know,' she acknowledged, anger fading to be replaced with sadness. 'It's just
that I love Marlin Bluff, and it hurts to hear people talking
of Marlin Bluff as a resort when it's still a community.'
Her grey eyes flashed a little. 'After all, Grandpa's still
preaching. We still live here.'

'No. Your sister lives in Port Douglas with her husband
and only visits here, and you...you live in New York.'

'Not now.' Her chin tilted. 'I live here now, and I live
at Marlin Bluff—not at Marlin Bluff Resort.'

'Very well, then.' Bryn spread his hands, giving in with
grace. 'For a month we'll admit that Marlin Bluff has a life
of its own outside this resort, but after that, when your
grandpa retires and the church is sold...'

'That's in the next Millennium,' Sophie said defiantly,
and managed another smile. 'Ages away—and you don't
own Marlin Bluff yet.'

Bryn grinned and nodded. 'Okay, Miss Connell, I'll
agree to that, but after the sale... As of January in the year
2000, I'm afraid this place will be mine.'

'As of the second of January,' Sophie said under her
breath. 'The first of January is Grandpa's.' But she smiled
straight back at him—a totally innocent smile—and out
loud she accepted.

'I'll agree to that, Mr Jasper. Bryn.' She wasn't going to
call him Mr Jasper. She wouldn't let this man intimidate
her! 'Bryn,' she repeated more firmly. 'But now, if you
want me to do some floral arrangements, then you'd best
show me the set-up, and if you want me to do some weddings, then I need to meet your brides.'

The first wedding was scheduled for the following day.

'I told you, I'm desperate,' Bryn told her as they walked
through the hotel to the florist workshop. 'It's the wedding

of Diana McInerney and Fred Hughes. Diana's father is okay, but his women…' He sighed. 'Well, "demanding" is too light a description for them. You'll meet them at ten.'

'There's a problem?'

'They were unimpressed by their trial bouquets. When I came back yesterday they were threatening to fly their own florist in.' Bryn grimaced. 'The McInerneys are very, very rich. Given the publicity this wedding's generating, that would be a disaster, so I gave you a bit of a promo.'

'What sort of a promo?' she asked cautiously, and he smiled.

'Nothing that isn't true. I set the publicity director to find anything she could on you. She gave Mrs McInerney a list a mile long of society weddings you've looked after.'

'Me?' Sophie fixed him with a look. 'Me, personally, or me and Rick? If you've done your homework you'll know I'm personally better known for my funerals.' She chuckled. 'I do a great wreath. You know, I can make one that can completely enfold a coffin, tasteful and all, and I've even picked out a name on top of a coffin in red, blue and gold everlasting daisies.'

'Very tasteful,' Bryn said faintly. 'You know, if I were you, I wouldn't tell Mrs McInerney that.'

'Why not?' Her eyes danced.

'How about because I'm your employer and I'm telling you not to?'

'Yeah?' She eyed him cautiously. To her surprise, he laughed. The autocratic moneymaker was taking a back seat.

'How about if I say please, then?' he asked, and Sophie caved in instantly. That smile… That laugh… They worked better than money, she thought. There was more than one form of power, and this man's smile could win him anything.

'Okay,' she conceded, and her voice was suddenly a trifle breathless. 'And you needn't worry; I can do weddings. It's just that Rick does most of them.'

'You mentioned Rick yesterday. Who's Rick?'

'My partner.'

'Your...?'

But there was no time for more. Bryn swung open the door of the workshop and stopped dead. The workshop was large—a huge room filled with tubs and stands of flowers— but it wasn't large enough. There were ten or so young women milling among the flowers, and a hugely bosomed matriarch booming fury at an unfortunate lady in a smock.

'Oh, no,' Bryn said faintly, and glanced at his watch. 'It's the McInerneys, *en masse*, three quarters of an hour early. This, Miss Connell, is your trial by fire.' He managed a smile across at the heaving bosom. 'Here we have mother, bride and bridesmaids,' he said, still in an undervoice. 'But mostly we have mother, and if you so much as mention an everlasting daisy—or a coffin—I swear you'll need them for yourself.'

Sophie grinned. This didn't faze her one bit. 'Mrs McInerney.' Pinning her brightest smile in place, she walked forward and took the bosom's hand. 'I'm so pleased to meet you. I'm Sophie Connell, Marlin Bluff's chief florist, and I'm sorry I haven't been able to meet you before, but I've just flown in from New York.'

Then she swung around until her gaze found the lady wearing the smock: middle-aged, blowsy blonde and with the air of a frightened rabbit. This, then, must be Bryn's florist's assistant. 'Louise,' she said warmly, in a tone suggesting they'd worked together for years. 'How's it going?'

Louise practically fell on her neck, and her voice was laced with tears as she held up a cream and yellow bouquet.

'It's not,' she confessed desperately, her eyes swinging

from Sophie to Bryn and back again, as if she was afraid she'd be sacked on the spot. 'Mrs McInerney told me to make another type of bouquet, and I did, but she hates it, so now she's saying Paul Jobier from Cairns is flying in to do the flowers.'

'Not in my resort, he's not,' Bryn said in an undervoice, but Sophie caught his words and cast him a compelling glance. *Shut up,* her glance said, and he did.

'Paul Jobier...' Sophie's gaze grew thoughtful. 'I know him. He exhibited in the international meets a few years ago when he was trying to make his name. He does very good work—not cutting edge now, of course, but still good.'

'He's better than this,' Mrs McInerney snapped. She wrenched the bouquet of pale lemon gladioli and iris from Louise's grasp and held it high. 'I said we wanted something dramatic and different. This is pathetic.'

'Gladioli are great for a tall look,' Sophie interrupted, casting a sympathetic, colleague-to-colleague glance at Louise. A florist's assistant should never have to face this sort of barrage, but half Sophie's working life was spent in public relations, and if she could get warring families to agree on coffin arrangements, then this should be a cinch. 'This is good, but if you want something more dramatic...'

Sophie paused and gazed around the room, assessing what was available. Hmm.

'If you don't like the gladioli, then maybe lilies could be used for a deeper yellow,' she said thoughtfully. 'I assume we're wanting golds? If so, do you know what would look really dramatic—and very Australian? If you'd like to get this wedding into international fashion magazines, why not use seed pods from the *typha domingensis*?'

She lifted a spike from a bucket at her feet. The brown seed pods resembled a smooth bean about eight inches

long, each pod set on a tall stem with a spike on top. They
were elegant, eye catching and stark in their simplicity.
Sophie twisted a pod into the bouquet, pulled the creamy
gladioli out and inserted deep gold lilies in their place, then
held the bouquet out, considering.

'Now it's elegant, but it's too harsh for a wedding. It'd
take the eye away from the bride. We need something else.'
She took gypsophila and wound it in at the back, trailing
it downward, then held it out again. Thirty eyes watched
every move.

'What do you think now?' she asked the heaving bosom,
who was eyeing her with acute suspicion. 'To my eye it's
striking and Australian and very lovely.' She turned to
Bryn, ignoring the hostility. 'If Miss McInerney doesn't
like this, and your next bride's agreeable, I suggest we use
it in the future. I'll send photographs to the columnists in
New York and I think we could get this featured…'

Then she paused, as if catching her thoughts. 'Oh, but
I'm getting carried away.' She turned back to the bosom.
'You were saying that you'd be asking Paul Jobier to do
your flowers, so this has nothing to do with you.'

'You know the fashion editors in New York?' Mrs
McInerney demanded, still glaring.

'Well, yes. I gather Mr Jasper's told you I usually work
from New York, and one does meet…' She caught herself
again. 'But that's hardly of interest if you've decided on
using Paul.' She smiled. 'If you'll excuse us, Louise and I
have work to do. And if you're having Paul do your flowers
then there's nothing…'

The bosom had ceased indignant heaving. 'I haven't decided yet,' the lady said.

'Mum, I love this.' A younger version of Mrs McInerney
spoke from the cluster of bridesmaids. The girl was twenty-
five or so, dark and lovely, but with a bosom that promised

future heaving, and the same mulish expression as her mother. Sophie felt a pang of sympathy for the unknown groom, and struggled to suppress a wince. 'I want to be in the international fashion magazines,' the young bosom demanded. 'I want this bouquet.'

The thing was decided.

'You were brilliant!'

Half an hour later, bosoms and bridesmaids had swept away to give the caterers a headache. Bryn stayed behind. 'Charles can handle them.' He grinned. 'If there's one thing my Gallic chef can do, it's handle women *en masse*, but you...'

'I know. I was brilliant.' Sophie turned to smile at Louise. 'It's not fair. The bouquet you did was lovely. It's only because they're looking for the limelight that they made so much fuss.'

'I never would have thought of your arrangement,' Louise admitted. 'To be honest, I didn't know what to do with those seed pods. Wendy ordered them before she left, but they look so ugly.'

'On their own they look ugly, but not in an arrangement. You know, that centrepiece in the main foyer would look great with about thirty of these spiking out.'

Bryn's smile broadened, and he gripped Sophie's hand with a warmth that flooded right through her. 'I can obviously leave you to it. Thank you, Miss Connell, for saving our butts. Name your rates. I'll pay.'

Maybe he would—but what form would that payment take? Sophie hesitated; she looked up at Bryn and paused. The feel of Bryn's hand holding hers and the look in his eyes did strange things to her. It made her feel as if the world had stopped and taken breath—and was waiting.

Waiting for what?

But Louise was watching with bright-eyed interest, and Bryn was smiling at her with an expression that said he was an employer satisfied with an employee and nothing more…and somehow she managed to pull her hand away.

'We'll…we'll talk about payment later,' she stammered 'At the moment…all I need is contact numbers for the rest of your brides so we don't have any more last-minute hiccups. I'll work through the list and see what I can arrange.'

'Up to the Millennium?' Bryn asked.

'Up to the Millennium,' Sophie told him. 'After that, you need to find yourself another florist.'

Because this one will be out on her ear, she told herself, and the thought was strangely bleak. Even if she'd wanted to stay, there was no way Bryn would want her after the Millennium—not after she'd taken back Grandpa's wedding.

All of a sudden, Jane Bond seemed awfully lonely.

CHAPTER FOUR

SOPHIE spent most of the day working on the flowers, and then she telephoned her month's brides. First she contacted all the brides with their weddings scheduled for the following week—after all, she was here to do a job—and then she contacted the two thousandth bride.

She'd hardly been able to control her face when Bryn had handed her the list with names. The two thousandth bride was Claire Lleyton, and she knew her! She remembered Claire from school as being a couple of years younger, dizzy blonde, indulged to the point of stupidity by rich parents, but basically kind-hearted. She could understand Claire marrying at Bryn's resort, in all its opulence, but, unless she'd changed since she was a child, she could also see the kind-hearted Claire changing her mind once she knew how much this wedding meant to John Connell.

To her delight Claire answered the phone herself, and she recognised Sophie at once.

'Oh, Sophie… How wonderful that you'll be doing my flowers. It's so exciting. Can you come here and see my dress?'

Certainly she could. If she intended backstabbing Bryn, she infinitely preferred to do it on neutral territory.

'Sure, Claire. I need to go into Port Douglas tomorrow and I'll be driving past your front door. I'll see you then.'

Sophie replaced the phone, turned—and found Bryn watching from the door.

'Isn't that taking things beyond the call of duty?' he

asked mildly, and she flushed bright crimson. If this man could read her mind, what then? Firing squad at dawn?

'What…what do you mean?' she managed.

'Claire could come here.'

'But I don't want to spend my entire holiday stuck in the resort. I'd far rather get out and about.'

Bryn considered this for a moment, then smiled, and Sophie was over her first hurdle.

'Do you have a car?'

'Grandpa lends me his.'

'I'll add a petrol allowance to your pay.' He smiled again, and her guilt grew to suffocation point. If she was intent on treachery, Bryn should be a bit nastier. How could she pinch his wedding if he turned out to be a friend? *Et tu, Brute…?*

But she wasn't out of the fire yet. *Brute* walked across and looked over her shoulder at her diary, and he frowned. 'The Lleyton wedding is last on your list,' he said slowly. 'You could put the arrangements off for a while yet.'

'If it's the Millennium wedding, it's the most important for your hotel,' she told him, forcing her voice to stay steady. 'The floral demands for the Millennium will be huge, and if you want this to be the wedding of all weddings, I need to get orders in now.'

'Very efficient.' He looked Sophie up and down with a smile that made her toes quiver. 'I can see why you're a success in New York—with artistic flair, public relations skills and efficiency as well.' His gaze deepened into a slow, lazy smile that was almost a caress, and Sophie's toes curled all by themselves. '*And* beautifully packaged, to boot. You'd better watch out. At the end of the Millennium I might not let you go.'

'Oh, you'll let me go all right,' she muttered, trying desperately to school her toes into behaving themselves. 'Believe me, Mr Jasper, as of the second of January, you'll be grateful to see the end of me.'

'I'm not so sure of that.' He paused, and the frown came back into his eyes, as if he was trying to figure her out. 'It's late now,' he said slowly, in a tone that said he wasn't sure what he was suggesting was sensible. 'Would you like to stay for dinner?'

'You mean have dinner with the staff? I... Thank you, but I need to go home.'

'I'm asking you to eat with me—not with the staff. We could have drinks by the pool, dinner in one of our restaurants, and afterwards I'll walk you home.'

That sounded just wonderful. She looked up into his eyes and was almost caught. Almost...

Good grief, no! She was here in traitor mode—to get what she wanted and then walk away fast! This man was dangerous—one look at him told her that. She could fall for Bryn in a big way, she thought wildly, and then winced inside at the knowledge of her own stupidity. How many other women had thought exactly what she was thinking about him? There must be thousands! The man was too good looking for his own good, too charming, and too...

Too Bryn!

Sophie took a deep breath and managed to shake her head with much more resolution than she felt. Inside, she was shaking all over.

'No, thank you, Bryn. Grandpa is cooking sausages, and I'm here to spend time with him. I'm sorry, but he comes first.'

Bryn's hawk-like look softened into understanding. 'All this and a heart as well,' he said softly, his lazy smile returning. 'Well, well. The package gets better.' His deep eyes flashed a twinkle. 'But you're here for a month,' he reminded her. 'Don't let your grandpa stock up on too many sausages. I'd like time to know you better between now and the Millennium.'

Whew… Maybe she ought to walk away right this minute!

Sophie spent a restless night coping with troublesome dreams, and woke up thinking of Bryn. She ate breakfast thinking of Bryn, and she drove to see Claire with Bryn's smile right in front of her.

Drat the man. Didn't he have more sense than to be nice to her? She was here to make herself the villain of the piece, so didn't he have the sense not to be so…so…?

So Bryn! She couldn't think of any other way to describe him. She was repeating the same thought over and over, and she was being a dope, but she couldn't help herself.

It was a subdued Sophie who knocked on the front door of the magnificent Lleyton residence, and by the time Claire answered Sophie had almost worked up enough guilt to turn and run. But then, how could she? Jane Bond's plot was in full swing. No matter where Claire's wedding took place, flowers had to be ordered and arrangements made, she told herself firmly, and if her smile was glassy as Claire opened the door, she was at least still standing there.

Claire didn't notice. She was just as Sophie remembered, blonde, bouncing, beaming, and enveloping Sophie in a bear hug like a long-lost friend.

'Sophie, this is fabulous. How wonderful that you'll do my flowers. I thought you were so terrific at school. You and Joe were two of my favourite people.'

'Me and Joe…'

'Oh, yes. You have no idea how much I wanted to tag along behind you. I was so jealous of your friendship.'

Jealous? Sophie blinked, and tried to think back through the years. Claire hadn't changed much since school. She was a blue-eyed bombshell now, and she had been then. Pretty, effervescent and rich, she had spent her school life surrounded by the in-crowd, and it seemed unlikely she'd even noticed Sophie and Joe—two older kids who had never been able to afford designer clothes and who had never aspired to be *in*.

But remember them Claire did, with a vengeance. 'How could I forget you after what you two did to my princess dress?' Claire said sternly, and Sophie blenched as Claire chuckled.

'Oh, heck, Claire, I was twelve years old…'

'Yeah, and I was ten, and I'd just been told I was Little Miss Marlin Bluff and I was to sit on the carnival throne and be gorgeous. I was *that* chuffed, even though I knew I ought to support Joe.'

'You were too young.'

'I was old enough to know the teacher was a cow. I can still remember Joe's face when she said he couldn't play his bagpipes in the procession because the scar on his face would upset everyone. You were so angry you said you wouldn't go in the procession either, and she looked down that crooked nose of hers and said, "Suit yourself, but you're being silly. You can organise the flowers."'

'I can't believe you remember this,' Sophie said faintly.

'Oh, I remember it.' Claire's dazzling smile flashed out and she chuckled. 'I sat on the float, being little Miss Princess in my gorgeous white dress, trying not to feel guilty that you and Joe weren't there, and then you presented me with the most magnificent bunch of tiger lilies…'

'We didn't…' Sophie blushed crimson.

'You did—as if you didn't know that tiger lilies' stamens spread a brown powdery stain like nothing else. I turned dirt-brown in about five seconds flat, and you and Joe were so innocent, no one would ever believe you knew the things stained.'

'Oh, Claire,' Sophie said weakly. 'I… It was just that I was wild with Mrs Holder. I'm sure we're both sorry. Do you forgive us?'

'Hey, of course—I forgave you years ago. I thought Mrs Holder was going to pop a valve, and that was much more fun to watch than me in a stupid fairy dress.' Then it was Claire's turn to blush. 'Though, actually, I had to forgive you,' she confessed. 'All through my teens I had the most enormous crush on Joe.'

'On Joe!'

'Yeah.' Claire shrugged and her smile faded. 'I know— it was silly. He didn't play his bagpipes in public after that, but I used to sneak around behind his mum's back fence and listen to him practise. I even asked him out once, but of course he wouldn't go. I'm too much of a dingbat for the likes of him.'

'I think…maybe you're too rich for the likes of Joe,' Sophie said softly. 'You know he and his mum were poor. He'd have been embarrassed to go out with you—and then there's his face. He's still so aware of it.'

'Well, that's stupid. He's the sexiest thing! I have fantasies about Joe with his bagpipes in a kilt…'

Sophie stared. What on earth was this? Joe in a kilt… 'Hey, Claire, are we talking marrying Joe, here, or are we talking marrying someone else?'

'Oh…' Claire's eyes widened as she hauled herself back to the present. 'Whoops. I have to remember I'm an engaged lady now,' she said hurriedly. 'That was all years ago, and of course now I'm marrying Colin, and Colin's really super. Come and see my dress.' Claire turned back into a bride, led Sophie into a side room, and Sophie was surprised all over again.

Claire was tiny, with huge blue eyes, a creamy complexion and soft, blonde hair which floated around her shoulders as a mass of curls. Sophie thought she'd look wonderful in a simple style that showed off her natural loveliness—maybe something shoulderless and sleeveless, with a tight-fitting bodice and a soft, sweeping skirt. She shouldn't wear a veil—just leave her lovely hair curling down to her shoulders and have a tiny riband of creamy roses threaded through.

But Claire's bridal finery was different from anything Sophie had imagined as suitable. Her dress was of embroidered satin with a padded bosom, low neckline, and wide sleeves sweeping down to gold-embroidered cuffs. It had a gilt-embroidered waistline and a skirt that must have taken twenty yards of heavy embossed satin to make. A train swung out ten yards behind, and there was a veil that stood up from a gold and diamanté tiara, and was just as magnificent as the dress.

You wouldn't *see* Claire in this dress, Sophie thought, stunned. She'd disappear. All you'd see would be the dress.

'Holy cow,' Sophie breathed before she could stop herself.

'Do you like it?' Claire asked anxiously. 'Colin chose it.' Then she hesitated. 'Sophie, I hate to waste your time, especially when you've driven all this way, but maybe Colin should be here when we choose the flowers. I thought he'd be here when I arranged this meeting, but he's been caught up on business. I always choose something that's too simple for his taste, and he thinks I'm stupid when I get things wrong.'

He thinks I'm stupid... Why was there suddenly a bad taste in Sophie's mouth? Sophie looked into Claire's worried face and felt a pang of doubt. Something was wrong here. What sort of loving fiancé would think his love stupid?

'Can't your parents help you choose? she asked.

'They're overseas,' Claire told her. 'They've been overseas for six months now. They're flying back the day before the wedding.'

'Do they like Colin?'

'Oh, yes. Daddy thinks he's a young man on the way up.' Claire giggled, her natural sunniness reappearing. 'They think I'm a dope and Colin is just what I need to settle me down. It's just a shame he's not here to meet you. He had to go to Cairns—there's a yacht for sale that he thinks will be great for our honeymoon. He came here this morning to have me sign papers and a cheque, but he could only stay for a minute…'

'He's buying the yacht with your money?' Sophie asked cautiously, and Claire shrugged.

'Well, yes. It has to be bought in my name because my money's in trust until I'm married. That's no problem, but I just wish…' Her voice trailed away…

Sophie was frowning. She spent her working life with people who'd just been bereaved or who were just getting married, and on both occasions emotions were raw. She was good at people, and her sixth sense told her things weren't right.

'You're not happy about the yacht?'

'Oh, I am. It's just that… I sort of thought we might be by ourselves on our honeymoon. But Colin's best man's coming from overseas with his girlfriend, and Colin says it'd be crazy if they came all this way and I didn't get to know them. He says if he…if *we* buy the yacht then they can join us, with a couple more of Colin's mates. It'll be one big party.'

'It sounds really romantic,' Sophie said dryly—and then she caught herself.

Don't interfere in other people's affairs, she told herself sternly. How many times had Rick drilled that into her? Her job was to supply flowers, not fix people's lives—so butt out, Sophie.

'Why did you decide to marry at the resort?' she managed.

'Oh, I didn't.' Claire's frown disappeared and the sun came out again. 'Colin and my parents did. They want so many people to come, and they thought it'd be impressive—a wedding on the first day of the new Millennium at the new resort.'

'I see.' Sophie took a deep breath. 'You didn't think of getting married in the old chapel, and having the reception at the resort afterwards? You used to come to Sunday School at Grandpa's church.'

The sunshine disappeared. An indefinable look of resignation washed across her face—as if Claire was a woman accustomed to not having her way. '*I* did think of it,' she admitted. 'I love the chapel, and I'm so fond of your grandpa that as soon as we were engaged I rang him and asked if he'd marry us. Then I realised Colin hated the idea, and my parents agree. They think the resort will suit their friends better.'

'I see.'

'The chapel's closing, after all,' Claire said, brightening again with a slightly forced smile. 'Your grandpa didn't mind when I told him, so it's just me being stupid—as usual. Mum, Dad and Colin tell me I'm an airhead all the time, so maybe it's just as well I'm marrying someone sensible.' She sighed, and shrugged. 'Never mind. What do you think, Sophie? Do you think it might be better talking to Colin about the flowers rather than talking to me?'

'Maybe I should talk to you both,' Sophie said cautiously, 'and…and when I do, maybe I can talk to you both about any other arrangements you're having doubts about.'

That was all she could do. She made an appointment for Claire and Colin to visit the resort the next day, but she drove away feeling more than a little disturbed.

At least she hadn't sabotaged Bryn's wedding yet, she thought. She could go back and face him without knowing the backstabbing was underway—enjoy him being nice to her for a while longer—and the thought made her shelve her misgivings about Claire. In fact, it gave her a warm glow from the toes up.

Drat the man! she thought savagely, as she nosed her car back Bryn-wards. Why did her thoughts keep turning straight back to Bryn?

'Tell me about Claire Lleyton,' she asked Grandpa over lunch.

'Claire Lleyton?'

'That's the one. Your two thousandth bride.'

'No,' John said firmly, pouring himself his second cup of tea. 'She's not my two thousandth bride. Claire's nothing to do with me. She's marrying at the resort, Sophie, and that's that.'

Sophie bit her lip but kept on. 'Just tell me about her. I hadn't heard of her since school.'

'She's a nice little thing,' John said. 'She lacks gumption, though. She wanted to go nursing, but her parents made such a fuss she finally abandoned the idea. Her mother's doing her best to turn her into a social butterfly. Claire does a bit of voluntary social work, to her mother's disapproval, and that's about all the independence she's allowed. Now her parents have matched her with this Colin Draffus…'

'You don't like Colin?' She almost didn't need to ask. John's bushy eyebrows were snapping together in distaste.

'He's an accountant-cum-property-developer in Port Douglas,' John said shortly. 'He's a pompous, money-grubbing twerp with the morals of a rather nasty form of pond scum.'

'Goodness.'

'Goodness doesn't come into it, but Claire can't see.' John sighed. 'Or she isn't allowed to see. Her father isn't any better, and her parents have pushed the match. Claire inherited quite a lot of money from her grandmother, Colin's her father's business partner, and this way the money gets to stay in the family firm.'

'Claire *was* the bride who cancelled the wedding here on the first of January?' Sophie probed gently.

'Well, yes,' John admitted. 'But I won't have you pressuring her to change her mind. She asked me if I'd marry her, and then Colin decided they'd marry at the resort. It wasn't even a firm booking.'

'So Bryn won your wedding…'

'It's not my wedding and Bryn didn't have anything to do with it.' John placed his hands on the table and leaned forward so he was facing her directly. 'Sophie, my time here is over. I'm no longer vicar in charge of St Marks because St Marks, as a church, is ceasing to exist. We've known it was inevitable any time these last two years and I don't want you implying it's Bryn's fault. That young man is simply filling a gap that I can't fill any more.'

'Grandpa…'

'Sophie, there's nothing more to be said. Leave it.'

Sophie left him with a mind going in all directions. It kept veering around and around Bryn, but Claire was in there too.

What I'd really like, she told herself, thinking of Claire's forced brightness, is to stick a spoke into this wedding so no one marries anyone—only that won't get Grandpa his two thousandth wedding. And you don't interfere with people's private lives, she reminded herself.

She sighed, but it was impossible to stop her mind plotting. But surely…if they are going to be married…the least they can do is use the chapel one last time. Surely it can't hurt anyone.

She looked along the beach and sighed again. She loved this place, and it was impossible to stay dismal in such a setting. Maybe she was imagining Claire's unhappiness. Happy endings were possible, after all, and for now she was on her way back to the resort—to see Bryn.

Goodness, things were getting complicated!

The McInerney wedding was scheduled for six, and Sophie arrived back at two to find Louise knee-deep in chaos. For the next few hours there was no time to think of anything besides lilies and seed pods and gypsophila and ribbon…

Finally the bouquets were delivered to the bridal suites. The last of the reception flowers were gaining their finishing touches as Bryn walked through the door, and Sophie's heart started racing all over again at the sight of him. He was wearing a dinner suit, and, in deepest black, was impossibly handsome…

Will you stop lusting after Bryn Jasper? she told herself crossly. Go pour a bucket of cold water on yourself. She struggled to her feet from where she'd been weaving ropes of rosebuds to be strung along the backs of the rows of seating, winced as her cramped muscles screamed a protest, stretched like a cat, and finally she smiled.

'Did you come in here dressed like that just so we can't give you a job?' she demanded, and Bryn's lazy eyes twinkled.

'That's right,' he agreed. 'It worked a treat when I was eight years old and it was my turn to muck out the poultry.'

'I don't believe it!'

'Well, it might have worked if I'd had a dinner suit when I was eight.' His smile deepened. 'The flowers are lovely, Sophie.'

To her chagrin, she felt herself blushing. 'Th…thank you.' Holy heck, she was stammering like a schoolgirl.

'The photographer from Cairns has just seen the bouquets and he's speaking in rhapsodies. He's never see anything like this before.'

'It's amazing what you can do when your back's against the wall.' She forced her attention to her last bucket of rosebuds waiting to be threaded. 'I… We're nearly finished. You can tell the boys they can take these rosebuds and hang them wherever they like.'

'You sound like you don't care where they hang them.'

'It's my job to arrange flowers.' She managed a grin. 'By the time I've arranged them, sometimes I'd like to tell people where I'd really like them put, and as for these rosebud ropes…'

'You don't like them?'

'They're twee,' she said crossly. 'Never mind. If the client demands pink rosebuds decorating the seating when everything else is in yellows, browns and gold, then what the client wants…'

'Is what the client gets.' He laughed. 'Spoken like a girl after my own heart—a true businesswoman.' Then his smile faded. 'What now, Sophie? Are you going home to Grandpa?'

'You don't need me after this, do you?' she asked, startled.

'No, but…'

'But?' For some reason her heart had started beating like a jackhammer—a very nervous jackhammer.

'I was wondering whether you'd like to come back later and have supper with me.' Bryn smiled, and his smile was coaxing. 'I understand you'd like to have dinner with John, but if I'm any judge, I'll bet he's in bed by nine or so. The night's lovely, but I'm caught up with this wedding until nine because our master of ceremonies has come down with flu. I thought…if you'd come back…'

He sounded absurdly unsure. It was as if it was Bryn who was in torn overalls, with foliage stains on his fingers and a guilty conscience to boot. Sophie looked up into his anxious face and suddenly there was no way in the world she could refuse him. 'About nine, then?' she asked, and she couldn't believe she'd just said it. What was she doing? She should be running a mile.

He nodded, his smile still anxious. 'The speeches should be over by then. I can disappear and my staff can take over everything else.' His smile enfolded her, that dangerous, endearing, lurking smile that had her heart doing handstands. 'The reception is out in the pavilion to the east of the swimming pool. Come there and find me. Please?'

Please… The word hung in the air between them, taut with meaning. If he hadn't said it, she might have been able to refuse. Maybe. But he'd said it—and there was nothing for her to do but to spread her stained hands and give in.

'That'd be lovely,' she heard herself say, and she couldn't believe what she was doing. 'I'll be there.'

She should have worn jeans and an old T-shirt when she returned to the hotel—or she shouldn't have gone at all. Instead, she changed into a dress.

The dress was bare-sleeved, softly collared, clinging at

the waist and falling in soft folds to just above her knees. The off-white raw silk dress was a lovely mix of formal and casual. Sophie used it often when she wasn't quite sure what was required. In this dress, if she ended up helping the staff with the washing up, she wouldn't look crazy, but if she ended up dancing under the stars with…

Stop it, Sophie! she told herself desperately. Get a hold on yourself.

By eight-thirty, Grandpa was fast asleep. She forced herself to wait until just before nine, then made her way down to the beach. The rain had stopped, the night was full of stars and it was only a few hundred yards along the beach to the hotel.

She'd gone about a hundred yards when three shadows emerged from the dark, but she didn't have time for nervousness before the tall shadow spoke.

'Sophie, it's me, Joe.'

She stopped dead.

'Is that…? Don't tell me…' She stood without moving while the shadows became reality. 'Good grief.' The two smaller shadows at the side of the taller one came into focus and they were unmistakable. Marty and Goggle!

To her amazement the dogs were following Joe without a leash between them. They walked peacefully down the beach towards her, then, at a click of Joe's fingers, they sat and waited for Joe's next order.

'Bryn guessed you might walk along the beach and he didn't want you walking alone,' Joe told her.

'So he sent Marty and Goggle to haul me safely to the hotel in bite-sized chunks. How thoughtful of him.'

Joe grinned, clicked his fingers again and they set off towards the hotel, the dogs beautifully in step behind. 'He knows I always walk the dogs at this time, and the beach is our favourite place,' he told her.

'You always walk the dogs…' Sophie slipped off her sandals and let her toes drift in the warm sand. 'I thought these were Bryn's dogs.'

'They are, but he's not here much.'

'Like…how much?'

'About one month in every six.' Joe grinned into the dark. 'It's not much time to train dogs.'

'Then why did he get them?'

'Same reason he keeps moving from one woman to another, I guess,' Joe said thoughtfully. 'He's not prepared to commit, but he wants a bit of loving and he gets it every way he can.'

'Yeah?' Sophie cocked her head to one side and thought about this. 'Joe Holloway, are you warning me?'

'I might be,' he said slowly. 'The man has ghosts in his past, Sophie.'

'Like who?'

'I don't know.' He spread his hands. 'But the rumour among the staff is that there's been some tragedy in his past and no woman is allowed near him. With his looks and charm, that makes him dangerous.'

'Hey, I've moved on since school,' she told him, startled. 'You remember me as fifteen years old with pigtails. I might have been a helpless schoolkid then…'

'You were never helpless,' Joe told her. 'That's about the last thing I'd describe you as. A more wilful, managing, scatterbrained…'

'Not your type?' she teased, and Joe shook his head with vigour.

'No way. Sorry, Sophie, but there it is.'

'So who is your type? Do you have a lady?'

There was silence, and all of a sudden the silence was uncomfortable.

'Joe...' Sophie bit her lip. 'Hey, Joe, I didn't mean to pry.'

'You're not prying.' He lifted a piece of driftwood and hurled it out into the waves. The dogs barked with joy and hurled themselves after it. 'I don't normally mind...'

'Mind what?'

He shrugged. 'Just that I don't have a "type"', he said bitterly. 'What woman goes out with someone as scarred as me?'

'Your scarring's sexy, and I would.'

He grinned. 'Yeah, maybe. But girls like you are different.'

'So what's wrong with girls like me?' She put her hands on her hips and glared.

'I can't imagine,' he said faintly. 'And I can't imagine why I thought of warning you about Bryn, but...'

'But I'm not your ideal woman?'

'I want a lady who's soft and caring and squishy round the edges.' Joe smiled into the dark—a bitter, self-mocking smile. 'She doesn't exist. Every girl I'm interested in either goes into mother hen mode—which I hate—or blanches and backs off in horror at my scarred face, which leaves me...'

'Still looking for the woman of your dreams,' she murmured, and tucked her hand into his. 'Joe, keep looking. She'll be out there somewhere, along with my Mr Right. Any minute now they'll come charging by on white horses...'

'As long as you don't reckon your Mr Right is waiting for you up at the resort wearing a dinner suit and preparing himself for the next lady in a long line...'

'Joe...'

He held up his hands.

'Okay.' He whistled the dogs and they fell obediently in

behind him. 'I've said what I wanted to say. Now I'll hold my peace and leave you to stuff up your life just however you please.'

'I won't stuff up my life.'

'You get emotionally involved with Bryn Jasper and he'll stuff it up for you.'

CHAPTER FIVE

Joe left her as they reached the grounds of the hotel.

'I'm not taking Marty and Goggle anywhere near a wedding,' Joe told her. 'I'm not saying they wouldn't enjoy it, but I reckon the guests might not enjoy them.'

Sophie could only chuckle and agree. She left him and made her own way to the pavilion.

The outer pavilion was empty. Sophie looked disdainfully at her ribbons of rosebuds hung along the seats. Ugh! Then she looked more dispassionately at the whole place. It *was* lovely, she decided. Open and light and filled with the sound of the sea, the building was hung with hundreds of yards of silk taffeta like huge white veils. It was beautiful—but Grandpa's chapel was better.

Claire needs to be married in the chapel, she told herself. Not here.

Claire doesn't need to be married at all.

Stop complicating your own plot, Jane Bond. She scowled. Go and find your villain.

Her villain was in trouble. Sophie reached the inner pavilion just as the bride's father rose to make his speech. Short, rotund and wobbly, he held a champagne glass in fingers that were none too steady—in fact he was shaking so much he was splashing champagne over his dinner jacket.

'Ladiesh and gentlemen,' he started. The champagne glass wobbled violently. 'Ladiesh…'

He took a deep, steadying breath, but it didn't steady him. It did the opposite. Bryn moved in fast behind as

Henry McInerney's knees buckled in a dead faint.
Somehow he managed to catch him, which left him standing before the microphone, with Henry's limp body in his
arms and about four hundred eyes staring straight at him.

Sophie wouldn't have moved for the world. She'd come
in a side entrance behind a screen used by the serving staff,
and she stared out at the scene in awed fascination. What
on earth would he do?

Mrs McInerney, resplendent in purple and with her
amazing bosom extended six inches further by a clutch of
pink roses, gave an angry gasp and rose to her feet—but
Bryn would have none of it.

'He's fine, ma'am,' he told her in a voice that was accustomed to command—to stopping people in their tracks.
'Leave him to me.' He lowered the unconscious Henry to
the ground, lifted a slip of paper from the man's limp hand,
straightened, and looked down at the paper for about twenty
seconds—then raised the microphone and began to speak.

'Ladies and gentlemen,' he said firmly. 'Henry
McInerney has asked me to convey his apologies for his
slight...' He paused and a smile twitched at the corners of
his mouth as he looked down at the recumbent Henry. 'His
slight attack of nerves.' The smile broadened. 'Emotion at
this great event—the marriage of a daughter—can cause
real stress in any man. For some it's overwhelming, but I
have here all the thoughts he'd like to share with you today.'

He smiled around at his audience, his smile telling the
guests that this was totally normal. *Daddy passing out at
daughter's wedding happens every day...* Mrs McInerney
slumped back into her seat, unsure now how to react.

That was one catastrophe averted, anyway. At least they
wouldn't have the mother of the bride smashing something
over the father of the bride's head, Sophie thought, and then

she was caught in Bryn's spell as he smoothly took over Henry's speech.

The speech was nothing less than masterly, and Sophie stood riveted. How could someone take one man's jottings—without knowing the family, without rehearsal, without even reading it beforehand—and turn it into a really superb speech?

In minutes he had the guests in turn laughing and wiping their eyes with emotion. On Henry's behalf, Bryn spoke of his love of his family and his daughter, his pleasure in her choice of husband, and his friendships, new and old. He welcomed the in-laws to the family, he told a couple of lovely jokes that had the guests eating out of his hand—he even managed to throw in a magnificent reference to the astounding purple frock his wife was wearing.

And at the end of the speech there was no way Mrs McInerney could feel anger towards her husband—not after the wonderful things that had been said about her. Bryn really did look as if he was reading straight from Henry's notes. She applauded with the rest of the guests, and Diana McInerney came from the bridal table and kissed her father soundly as Bryn and one of the waiters lifted him to take him outside.

'You take good care of him,' the bride quavered, not quite sober herself. 'To write a speech like that... Oh, Daddy, I've never heard you speak like that.'

Behind the screen, Sophie was feeling emotional herself—in fact her heart was tying itself in knots. This man was something else! She'd never met a man like this.

'And did Daddy speak like that?' Sophie demanded, as she followed into a back room and watched as Bryn laid Henry on a settee.

'Well...' Bryn straightened, glanced down at the crumpled piece of paper in his hand and carefully ripped it into shreds. 'Goodness knows.' He grinned. 'I couldn't read any more than a few names.'

'So it was your speech!' Sophie smiled back, her heart doing silly backflips. 'It's you who Diana McInerney should be kissing.'

'Heaven forbid.' Bryn tugged off his tie and unfastened the top button of his shirt, which made him look far more casual—and even sexier than he'd been before! His dark eyes gleamed with laughter and her hormones started doing things they'd never thought of doing in their lives. 'But if we're speaking of people I'd rather kiss... Dan, can you organise champagne and chocolates out at the poolside?' And he took her arm in a hold that was entirely possessive.

Oh, Lord...

Joe had warned Sophie Bryn Jasper would stuff up her life, and as he took her arm in his and led her out into the night, she knew Joe was exactly right.

Grandpa's chapel might be better than Bryn's wedding centre, but nothing beat his swimming pool. Sloping gently to deep water, it was lined with wide ribbons of sand and lit underneath by hundreds of turquoise lights that sparkled and glittered in the moonlight. A band was playing somewhere inside the hotel and the soft music was drifting across the water, acting as a magical backdrop to the sound of the ocean, only yards away.

Sophie stared around her in stunned silence as Bryn released her arm. There was no one else in sight. A table had been set with soft white linen and two crystal champagne flutes, and there were two plush chaise longues, side by side, just waiting for occupants.

This was some seduction scene!

'You set this up,' she said accusingly, and Bryn grinned.

'I'm a man who likes to be prepared.'

'Obviously!' She couldn't think of anything more to say. Her body temperature was rising by the minute. In desperation, she slipped off her sandals and walked ankle-deep into the water. He made her temperature rise just by looking at her!

There was a sand island five yards out, built as a play area for children, and a bucket and spade lay abandoned from the day's play. Trying to break the rising tension, she bent down and inspected the contents of the bucket—and her eyes widened as she saw what it contained. The small owner of the bucket had obviously made a few trips to the beach today.

She turned to show Bryn, but he was still watching her with a strange, speculative smile, and a frisson of electricity was charging back and forth between them like crazy. The seduction scene was almost overwhelming, and for the moment the bucket in her hand was forgotten. 'Do you…do you own all of this?' she asked from the safety of her island.

Bryn laughed. 'Hell, no.' His eyes watched her, calmly waiting. It was as if he was getting the preliminary conversation out of the way before the serious business of lovemaking began. 'I'm just the major shareholder.'

'So you own fifty-one per cent?'

'Something like that.'

'And fifty-one percent of…how many other hotels?'

'Six, worldwide.'

'I see.' She managed a chuckle, but she didn't feel much like laughing as she looked back at him across the shallows. This man was way out of her league. 'At least, I don't see. I can't imagine how it must be to have so much money under your control.'

'And so many people,' he added, his voice serious. 'That's the hard part.'

'You don't like hiring and firing?'

'Hiring's great.' His eyes glinted across at her. 'I mean, look who I pick up when I hire?'

Damn him, he was seducing her with his eyes! Somehow she forced herself to concentrate on practicalities.

'But if I stop saying yes, sir; no, sir, three bags full sir, then you'll fire me?'

'You'll leave me anyway,' he said mournfully. 'Come the Millennium and you'll head back to New York without a backward glance.'

'Do you have a hotel in New York?' Now why had she asked that? She flushed in the dim light and hoped like crazy he hadn't noticed.

'No,' he said, and his voice grew even more mournful. 'Hey, but I could always buy one.' He grinned and cheered up, sinking his long frame onto a chaise longue as Dan appeared with an ice bucket and champagne. Dan looked from Sophie to Bryn, his face impassive as he set down his tray. He allowed himself a small, non-committal smile as Bryn thanked him, and then he took himself serenely away. 'Would you like that, Sophie?' Bryn asked, continuing where he'd left off. 'Would you like me to buy a hotel in New York?'

As a seduction line, this was pretty breathtaking. Moonlight and champagne and millionaires offering to buy hotels in her back yard... She appeared to consider, but the scene was sending her way right out of control.

He was expecting her to get out of the water and sit beside him, but she didn't dare go one inch closer, she decided. 'So you can visit me once every six months?' she managed at last, in a voice that was decidedly unsteady. 'Like you do your dogs.'

'Well...'

'You know, you shouldn't have bought your dogs,' she told him in a schoolmarm tone, and he grinned.

'Maybe not. They were a whim. My mother told me I needed something to love so I bought them.' He brightened. 'But, hey, Joe loves them, and they're two thoroughly nice dogs. Sophie, come and sit down. These are really comfortable.'

She glared. 'You've managed to shelve your canine responsibilities nicely. What do you do with the rest of your responsibilities?'

'I give them to my mother,' he said, so promptly that she was forced to laugh, but then his tone grew serious. 'But what do you mean by my responsibilities? Do you mean the people I fire? Believe me, I never do that without soul-searching.'

'You must be ruthless, though, to have made so much money.'

'I had a bit to start with,' he confessed. 'My father…'

'I know. Your father ran La Ville in the south of France.' That much she'd read about him. 'But you've moved on from there.'

'I don't like standing still,' he said slowly. 'I never have.'

'You mean you'll never settle down?' She was standing on her island with her gruesome bucket in her hand and she felt weird and spacy—as if time was being held in limbo. 'You'll never have time for…'

'For responsibilities?' He grinned. 'There's reproof in your tone, Sophie Connell. You want me to stay here and train my dogs?'

'If you want them to love you,' she said with asperity. 'They love Joe now.'

'Well, maybe that's a good thing,' Bryn said reflectively. 'Joe could use some loving. Sophie, come here.'

Sophie stayed right where she was, her toes digging into

the sand as if she needed to get a grip. 'Did Dan's funny smile mean we'll be talked of all over the resort tomorrow?' she managed, and Bryn shook his head.

'Nope.'

'You mean he's used to you being with women? Boss of the world with one beautiful woman after another?'

'Well, it beats being with men,' Bryn retorted, and rose to his feet. 'Sophie, I'm hearing a distinct note of moralising in your tone. Why are you standing out in the water when the champagne's here?'

'Because this scene looks like something out of a how-to-seduce-a-woman manual,' she said with asperity. 'I have a feeling this scene's been tried before.'

'Sophie…'

'I'm right, aren't I?' She didn't have to ask. Bryn's startled tone told her she'd hit the nail right on the head. 'I think I should go home,' she said softly. 'I'm not here to be seduced.'

'What are you here for?'

I'm here to take your wedding…

The thought flashed into her head and scared her senseless.

'I *was* here to have supper with you,' she said stiffly. 'That doesn't mean I intend to fall into your arms.'

'You don't want to be kissed?'

Did she? She stared blankly across the water to where he was standing. His dark eyes gleamed in the moonlight, teasing and tantalising and daring her to come to him, and suddenly she knew what her answer was. Yes! All she wanted to do was to walk out of the water, let him take her into his arms and kiss her senseless.

She was senseless already, she thought wildly. For heaven's sake, she was here to help Grandpa, not to become another name on this man's list of conquests.

'Sophie…'

Remember Grandpa! she told herself desperately, as Bryn spoke her name in a way that made her legs turn to jelly. She owed John such a lot. Think about it!

Sophie and Ellie had been tiny when their parents were killed, and John had been on his way to becoming a bishop. After their deaths, he had stayed on as Marlin Bluff's vicar and never once had he alluded to lost ambitions.

John deserved a wonderful retirement celebration, Sophie thought fiercely—forcing her thoughts desperately away from the sight of Bryn's body—and he wouldn't get one unless she could win him the Millennium wedding.

But Bryn's gaze was making everything fuzzy. His eyes were troubled, as if he really cared, and that caring was close to her undoing. 'What is it, Sophie?' he asked, as he watched the confusion playing over her face.

'I don't…'

'You don't know whether you want to be kissed?'

'No. Yes! I don't know…' Her voice was practically a wail, and then she froze as Bryn kicked off his shoes and headed straight for her. 'Bryn, no…'

'Because I really want to kiss you,' he said softly, his eyes not leaving her face as he strode out through the shallows. 'I've wanted to since the first time I saw you; so, Sophie, if you don't want to be kissed, then you're going to have to give me a pretty firm refusal.' And he took two more steps forward.

She did. Sophie did the only thing she could think of. She lifted her bucket and hurled the contents straight at him.

It was a pretty sobering moment. The bucket had been filled to the brim with transparent blobs of jellyfish, washed up and collected from the shoreline. This type of jellyfish was totally harmless, and fascinating to children, but, though picked up firm and whole, they'd started to melt in the day's sun and were now reduced to a pulpy, jelly-like mass. They caught Bryn fair square across the face, stayed blob-like for an awful, endless moment—and then dripped slowly down across his shirt and jacket and into the water beneath him.

Oh, help…

'Bryn, I'm so sorry…' Sophie's hand flew to her mouth, aghast. Bryn stood motionless while the globs dripped off him and Sophie bit her lip. Then she bit it harder and the corners of her mouth twitched.

'If you dare laugh…' he said conversationally, staring down with disbelief at the descending blobs.

'You'll sack me?' It was too much. Sophie chuckled and her eyes danced with mischief. 'I'm sorry, but you did say you needed a firm refusal.'

'A nice, polite no would have been adequate.' Bryn wiped the last blob from his cheek, looked down in disgust at his hand and then let his eyes drift back to Sophie. 'But you didn't say it. Now I wonder why?'

'Bryn…'

He took two menacing steps towards her—she gave a yelp of fright and dived straight into the deeper water behind her island.

If there was one thing Sophie could do it was swim. She and Ellie had swum like fishes since they were tiny, and the fact that she was wearing a dress made no difference at all. The sliver of her silk dress seemed to disappear as her body knifed down to torpedo underwater for maybe twenty yards—then she broke the surface and started stroking steadily away.

Where?

Anywhere, she thought. This pool was huge, surrounding the entire hotel. The water was sun-warmed and glorious and her emotions were heating her body through and through. She needed to do something—anything—and to put her head down and stroke through the water as though a shark was behind her was an absolute relief. He'd never catch her.

He did. Bryn caught her at the third bridge. He stroked on in rhythm with her for another hundred yards and then simply used his larger body to herd her sideways into shallow water. Finally she was beached, floundering in the shallows and trying to rise. Bryn's hand came out and gripped her wrist and she was hauled back into the water without ceremony.

'I'll yell,' she spluttered down at him. 'I'll have every one of your guests out here...'

'Sophie.' His arm came around her and held in a grip of iron. 'You threw jellyfish at your boss and *you're* threatening to yell? Are you really telling me you don't want to be kissed?'

'Bryn...'

He grinned wickedly in the moonlight. '"Bryn" doesn't mean *no*. Lady, I said say no and all you offered was jellyfish. I don't understand jellyfish. Say no if you mean no. It's your last chance.'

She tried to frame the word as he laughed down at her. Her mouth opened but no word came out.

What was happening to her? She had no idea. All she knew was that she'd never felt like this in her life before, and she could no sooner resist this man than she could fly. She had to say no—but her voice, when she finally managed to get it to work, betrayed her completely.

'Bryn,' she whispered, and it was a plea all in itself.

'Are you sorry you threw a bucket of jellyfish at me?' he said fiercely, his eyes still laughing as he tilted her chin so her eyes were forced to meet his.

She choked and said the word at last. 'No.'

'That's what I thought.' He hauled her in tighter so they were sitting waist-deep in the water and her soaking body was cradled against his. 'You're wicked and unrepentant and altogether unmanageable. If I let you go, would you do it again?'

'I might.' There were shards of warmth shooting up and down her body. She felt deliciously alive—tingling all over—just waiting…

'Then there's nothing for it. I can't let you go until you're suitably punished.' He looked down at her for a long, long minute—and then slowly—tenderly—as though she was a precious and lovely thing and this wasn't a scene he played out night after night in every one of his fabulous hotels scattered throughout the world—he kissed her.

Quite simply, it changed her life. The kiss was long and lingering and lovely, and somewhere in the midst of this first kiss, Sophie learned that her world could never be the same. She'd never been kissed like this—not once in her twenty-eight years. Bryn's lips, his searching tongue, his hands caressing the soft curves of her body—the whole of him—made her feel as if something inside her heart was melting.

Her body was melting and he was all she wanted. She was a part of this man and he was a part of her—two people fusing into one.

Only, of course, that was stupid, because as the kiss ended, as all kisses finally must, she was left staring stupidly at her love, and she knew that what she was feeling was impossible.

Behind Bryn was his multimillion-dollar resort hotel. Around them were three acres of swimming pool. He owned a mile or so of prime beach frontage at Marlin Bluff, he owned the same amount of property in six other countries in the world, and she'd seen his picture in how many society tabloids?

She knew him because she'd seen him photographed with one beautiful woman after another, and here she was, melting into him, kissing him—and becoming yet another scalp for his belt.

Dear heaven, she couldn't walk away unscathed if she went any further—in truth, she couldn't walk away unscathed now—and if she let this man take her, as her body was screaming that it wanted, then she'd cling like glue and never let go.

He was looking gravely down at her, laughter gone. 'What is it?' he asked softly. 'Sophie…' And he pulled her gently into his arms to kiss her once more.

'Bryn, no.' Somehow she managed to pull away. She pushed herself back from him in the shallows and fought for words to explain the unexplainable.

A shadow appeared on the shoreline and Sophie almost gasped in relief. It was Dan, his impassive face even more impassive as he took in the sodden couple sitting out in the pool. They were three hundred yards from where he'd left them, and heaven knew how he'd found them now. Maybe half the occupants of the hotel had looked out of the windows and seen that kiss…

Maybe it didn't matter, Sophie thought bitterly. Maybe Bryn's staff were accustomed to watching Bryn's seduction scenes. Certainly Dan's face said there was nothing unusual about this.

'Excuse me, miss,' he told her calmly. 'There's an urgent call from New York. Someone by the name of Rick Hastings wants to speak to you.'

'Rick!' Sophie forced herself to focus on something other than Bryn, and somehow rose to her feet. 'How…how did Rick know I was here?'

'He rang your grandfather, and your grandfather gave him this number.' Dan looked from Bryn to Sophie, and his voice was apologetic—it also contained a trace of suppressed laughter. 'He was insistent he speak to you straight away, miss, or I wouldn't have disturbed you. You can take the call just through the first door, if you will.'

'I'll come,' Sophie said unsteadily. 'Thank you.'

'Rick?' Bryn asked, as she pushed herself to her feet and dripped down on him. 'Do I know Rick?'

'I told you about Rick,' she managed. Then a wild idea occurred to her, and before she could think about it she was using it. 'Rick's my partner,' she told him slowly, letting her voice dwell on the word 'partner' with affection. 'So you see, I have no right to seduction by moonlight. Thank you very much for the swim, Mr Jasper. The kiss was very nice, and I'm sorry about the jellyfish—but I'll take the call, and then I'd best be going home.'

Whew!

Sophie lifted the receiver and spoke to Rick, aware Bryn was still watching her through the windows as she dripped water onto the foyer floor. She forced a smile, and when she spoke it was with wholehearted delight.

'Rick, love…'

'Sophie?' Rick's voice was blank. 'Is that you?'

'Of course it is.' She let her smile slip a little. 'What's wrong?'

'Sophie, Mabel Fortingue died yesterday.'

'Mabel…' Her brain clicked into gear as she pushed herself harder to block out Bryn. Rick was half a world away, in another life. 'Oh, right. I remember. She's the wife of Ted Fortingue, who died last year. Well, she was in her nineties, Rick. It's hardly a disaster.'

'Yes, but it is.' Rick's voice moaned down the phone.

'Sophie, you remember the flowers you did for Ted's coffin?'

Oh, right. She choked with laughter, knowing what was coming. 'Yep. Ted's was the funeral where I did the everlasting daisies, with his name picked out...'

'She wants the same,' Rick wailed. 'At least her family do. They say you did such a wonderful job that they want a repeat—a whole coffin draped in everlasting daisies with her name woven through, and they want stars and stripes to boot.'

'It sounds really special.' It was hard keeping her voice deadpan, and Rick heard the laughter.

'Sophie...'

'Rick, I'm sure you're up to it.'

'Sophie, come back.'

'Not until after the Millennium,' she said sweetly, smiling her most loving smile and turning so she made sure Bryn could see it. 'And not until you've done your fair share of funerals, Rick. I'm sure you'll be more than up to picking out stars and stripes in everlasting daisies, and I'll really enjoy the thought of you doing it.'

Carefully she replaced the receiver. Poor Rick. For a moment she felt a pang of guilt—but only for a moment. If she'd been there, Rick would have pulled rank or age and made her do the dratted thing, while he flitted off to do another wedding, but Sophie was gloriously half a world away. He could do the coffin and she'd stay here and do her weddings.

But...if that was all she had to do it would be fine.

She looked outside to Bryn and she felt her heart twist. Bryn's face was questioning and searching, gentle and wondering. He didn't look the seducer at all.

Things weren't fine here. Things were very, very complicated.

CHAPTER SIX

SOPHIE spent a sleepless night before returning to the resort mid-morning. A large part of her didn't want to go near the place—there was a voice telling her to run straight back to Rick and his funerals and his everlasting daisies—but she'd had breakfast with her grandfather and his pleasure in her company had steadied her.

'I'm so glad you've come back before I have to leave here,' he'd told her. 'Just spending time here with you is lovely.'

'What's happening to this place after you leave?' What Ellie was pushing at the moment was that John would move into their large home at Port Douglas. Sophie knew John had reservations, but there seemed little alternative. At least Ellie lived near the beach and John could keep his dogs.

'There's an auction here in January,' John had said. 'Not that it'll make much difference. The whole place will be swallowed by the resort.'

'Is it certain? Surely if there's an auction...'

'Bryn will buy it. He owns all of the headland apart from this piece, and no one can afford to outbid him.'

'Why doesn't he buy it before the auction?'

'He's a businessman, Sophie,' John had said heavily. 'There's a price on it for prior sale but it's steep. Bryn knows he'll get it cheaper if it goes to auction.'

So not only was he pinching Grandpa's wedding, he was penny-pinching into the bargain! Sophie's prickles bristled now, and she walked into the hotel with spurts of anger helping her along.

She saw him briefly while she was perched on a ladder doing the foyer's floral arrangement—he came out of his inner sanctum with two Chinese businessmen by his side.

'Good morning, Sophie,' he said blandly as he passed underneath her ladder. 'The pants of my dinner suit have shrunk by two inches and they stink of fish. Is it okay if I deduct the cost from your wages?'

'I'll have you up for sexual harassment if you do,' she said sweetly, smiling at the men accompanying him as if she was talking about the weather. 'Seducing female employees... Serving hard liquor to innocent maidens...'

'Innocent maiden, ha! And there's jellyfish clogging up my filtration system.'

'Innocent maiden,' she repeated, grinning as she stuck another lily in her arrangement. 'And I'm sure your filtration system can cope with a few jellyfish. Aren't you going to introduce me to your companions—or don't employees rate introductions?'

Bryn's eyebrows hit his hairline. This was not the way his employees usually talked to him. 'I'd introduce you,' he told her, 'but my companions have no English. Unless you speak Mandarin...'

In answer, Sophie gave him her very best 'employee dismissing idiot boss, and isn't it nice that ladders make one feel immeasurably superior?' smile—and then she twisted so she was again smiling down to the Chinese.

'Nimen hao,' she said softly. *'Huan ying Ao da li ya.'*

The businessmen's faces lit with pleasure as she welcomed them to Australia. 'You speak Chinese?' the older of the pair asked in Mandarin, and she answered in the same.

'A little,' she told them. 'I have many friends from your country.'

'And you work here, yes?' The older man paused. 'I

wonder…would you share a meal with us?' He glanced at his younger compatriot. 'Apart from Mr Jasper, there is no one here who speaks our language.'

Sophie smiled and nodded. 'That would be lovely. How about joining me for lunch today?' She carefully avoided Bryn's eyes as she went on in slow, careful Mandarin, 'I've just come from the United States and I'm lonely, too. My name is Sophie. Contrary to what Mr Jasper believes, names don't need translation.'

Bryn practically gaped. 'Sophie…'

'Bryn, if you'll excuse me,' she said, reverting to English. 'I really am very busy. May I meet you in the Morton Bay room at twelve?'

'I have another appointment at twelve,' Bryn told her, glowering darkly, and his tone was dangerous.

'That's fine.' She gave him another sweet smile, turned again to the two men and reverted to Chinese. 'We can manage by ourselves. We don't need Mr Jasper.'

Which was fine—but why had her knees turned to jelly on her ladder? Bryn swept his charges away and Sophie had to take three deep breaths and then find herself a strong cup of coffee before she could climb her ladder again.

As for Bryn… He tried to perform contract negotiations with the Chinese—they had four business delegations due here over the next year and needed to negotiate rates—and all he could think of was Sophie.

Sophie in her cute little overall, perched on her ladder.

Sophie launching into near perfect Mandarin.

Sophie smiling.

She'd thrown jellyfish at him, he told himself desperately. She made mud angels with her body, she gave him cheek and she had this phantom Rick in the background. She was a nut, and a nut who was spoken for.

So get a hold on yourself, he told himself, and hauled his mind back to the matter in hand—with little success. Good grief, Jasper, she's just an employee.

There was no room in his life for the way he was feeling. Hadn't he told himself over and over that there was no way he ever wanted to be involved with a woman again? To love a woman as he'd like to love Sophie... It still seemed a betrayal, and it would open him to the same searing hurt...

So... *She's just an employee!*

But he already knew that Sophie was far more than that.

Bryn's Chinese delegation meant he was occupied when Sophie met Claire and Colin. The couple arrived promptly at eleven to organise their flowers, but they did nothing to settle her shattered nerves. She disliked Colin at sight.

The man wore a three-piece suit! Any male wearing a three-piece suit in thirty-five-degree heat was necessarily suspect, and Colin was just plain awful. He patronised Claire as he would a child.

Sophie had dressed up for him. Suspecting from Claire's and her grandfather's descriptions just what sort of man he was, she'd brought clothes over to the resort, changing out of her overalls for the interview and greeting Colin and Claire at her sophisticated best. Her chic red suit was immaculately cut and fitted her body to perfection, her curls gleamed in unaccustomed order and she was wearing 'knock-out' make-up, with scarlet lipstick to match her suit. She'd topped—or bottomed—the outfit with stilettos that, when she'd first bought them, she'd had to practise with for hours before she could balance without a wobble.

This was an outfit she reserved for making an impression, and make an impression she did. Colin's eyes nearly started out of his head.

Claire, however, hardly noticed. In Colin's presence, she had lost her bubble. Colin did all the talking—and he talked! It took fifteen minutes before Sophie could get a word in edgeways.

'Let me show you my folio,' she told him finally. 'It may give you some ideas…'

Her folio was designed to impress, consisting of photographs taken at her most prestigious functions, with each cut from one of New York's leading glossies. Colin was clearly taken aback. He fingered the shiny paper of each photograph and Sophie could see the longing in his eyes.

She hadn't been mistaken, then—this man was hungry for money, power and publicity. Bryn could give him publicity, but maybe he hadn't stressed just how much publicity the Millennium wedding would generate. If she could get in first…

'This is amazing.' The folio almost had Colin silenced, but not quite. 'Do you think…I mean, would you doing our flowers get our photographs into one of these?'

She had him! This was Mrs McInerney all over again—but she smiled ruefully and shook her head.

'I don't think so.' She sighed. 'The flowers would be good enough, and of course Claire's dress is wonderful, but the whole thing has to have an angle to interest an editor.'

'I thought getting married on the first day of the Millennium was angle enough.'

'No.' Sophie shook her head and tried not to dwell on what her grandfather thought of people who bent the truth. 'Not when you consider there's goodness knows how many resorts in the world and all of them will be trying to have a Millennium wedding.' She sighed apologetically. 'The problem is that you and Claire aren't exactly well known.'

'Claire's family is rich.'

'Sure, and they're influential here, but not overseas. Now

if there was something more…' Sophie left a pregnant pause, as though considering. 'I can't understand why you cancelled the wedding ceremony at Marlin Bluff Chapel.'

Colin frowned. 'We wouldn't get publicity there,' he growled. 'It's just an old church.'

'It's the most beautiful old church in Queensland,' she told him, straining hard to keep her voice calm. 'It's the sort of setting international editors would fall over themselves to photograph. And did you know it would be Father Connell's two thousandth wedding, and his last before he retires?' She sighed romantically. 'With a story like that, and in that setting, I wouldn't be surprised if you featured in every newspaper and magazine in the country. Plus overseas…' She smiled her most innocent smile. 'We'd just need to contact a few editors and let them know.'

'How…?'

'I could do that.' Heavens, how hard it was not to appear eager!

'But we've booked the wedding here now,' Claire said, her voice bewildered. 'And my parents…'

'Don't be stupid,' Colin snapped. 'I'll talk your father around.'

'You could still have the reception here.' Sophie took a deep breath and threw in a final inducement. 'If you use the chapel, I'll do the flowers for free.' Then, as Colin flashed her a suspicious look, she managed an innocent smile. 'I could use the publicity myself,' she told him. 'Here, the resort management get the credit for flower arrangements. At the chapel, I personally get publicity.'

'But, Colin…' Claire shook her head in confusion, then caught herself as Colin frowned at her. 'I'm sorry. Of course I'd like to be married at the chapel, but it's just… You know I don't think as fast as you. Look, why don't I take a walk while you and Sophie organise the flowers? You don't need me.'

Once more, Sophie felt a guilty lurch in her stomach. Was she organising something here that Claire didn't want? Surely not, she told herself. Claire was a big girl now— certainly old enough to know whether she wished to be married or not.

'Excuse me, Sophie…'

She whirled with a guilty start, half expecting to see Bryn behind her. Instead it was Joe, bearing an armload of palm fronds.

'Louise told me you needed these,' he said. 'We were doing a trim around the pool this morning.'

'Yes. Thank you.' It was *so* hard to get the guilty colour from her face! What on earth was she doing here? Sophie looked at Colin and saw dollar signs and ego in his eyes. She looked at Claire and saw confusion and a trace of un- happiness.

'Joe, are you frantically busy?' she asked, and Joe shook his head.

'Nope. I'm just off to check the beach has been cleared. We had seaweed wash in during the night and I set a couple of youngsters to clear it.'

'Would you…would you mind taking Claire with you for half an hour?' Sophie asked. 'She wants a walk. Would you like to do that, Claire? Is that okay with you, Joe?'

'It's fine by me.' Joe cast a surprised look at Claire, and his eyebrows rose in query—then he looked more closely as he recognised her. 'Hey, if it isn't Claire Lleyton from school. Is something wrong?'

'No,' Sophie said firmly. It couldn't be. Jane Bond would let nothing stand in her way—not even an uncertain bride. After all, she told her conscience, Claire and Colin were getting married anyway. There was no way she could stop them, no matter what she thought of Claire's intended. 'Colin and I are talking wedding plans,' she told Joe, 'and I think Claire is getting a touch of pre-wedding nerves. Would you like to check out seaweed instead of talking wedding, Claire?'

'Oh, yes, please.' Claire brightened immediately and she flashed her gorgeous smile at Joe. 'Joe. How lovely.' Her voice firmed. 'I think this is a good idea, Sophie. Changing things, I mean. It'll make it seem more of a real wedding.' Then she looked directly at Sophie. 'I trust you to arrange me a wedding I'll love.'

Should anyone trust her? Sophie was starting to think she shouldn't even trust herself.

'So what are you changing?' Joe asked mildly a couple of hours later. 'With Claire's wedding, I mean.'

Sophie took a deep breath. 'Claire and Colin are thinking of changing the wedding so they have the ceremony at the chapel and the reception at the resort. Colin's thinking about it. He'll let Bryn know when he's decided.'

Joe stopped short. He'd been walking back along the track with her, Marty and Goggle at his side.

'Are you kidding?' he asked faintly. 'Bryn will kill you!'

'Yep.'

He stared down at her. 'Does he know yet?'

'They haven't decided for sure,' Sophie said defensively.

'But you're working on them?'

'Yes.'

'I see.' Joe bit his lip and a faint smile pulled at the corner of his mouth. 'I begin to see a whole heap that wasn't otherwise clear. Sophie Connell, you haven't changed a bit. You always were a scheming, Machiavellian little…'

'I was not,' she said hotly.

'You were, too. Remember Claire's Little Miss Marlin Bluff bouquet…

Sophie blushed, but glared. 'I was twelve years old and it was half your idea.'

'It was not. I just tagged along, as I did with all your mad schemes. Of all the rotten things to do…'

'She didn't mind,' Sophie said. 'She thought it was funny.'

'She always was a good-natured little thing.' Joe hesitated, and his voice grew grave. 'Sophie, be careful. Playing with Bryn Jasper is like playing with fire.'

'I'm not playing with Bryn.'

'You are,' he said definitely. 'I have eyes in my head.' Then his voice grew softer. 'And you be careful of Claire,' he said, and there was a hint of steel in his voice. 'I might have tagged along in your wild schemes in the past, but Claire isn't a pawn in some game.'

'I never said she was.'

'She's just a kid.'

'She's twenty-six years old!'

'And she's been pushed around enough in her twenty-six years,' he said firmly. 'Her parents are autocratic snobs and Colin's just the same. Anyone can see that, but she's too kind-hearted to stand up to them. If you and Bryn make her the meat in your sandwich…well, if I have to stand in your way, then I will.'

'Goodness…'

'Goodness is right,' he told her. 'There'd better be goodness in all of this, Sophie Connell. You have a good heart. I expect you to use it.'

Her guilt was threatening to overwhelm her. Sophie left Joe where the track forked to the chapel, but instead of going home she headed for the beach and spent an hour walking

along the shallows. She might have water only to her an-
kles, but she was wading in over her head, she thought
bitterly, kicking salt water up before her, and for the life
of her she didn't know what to do.

Should she abandon everything and head back to New
York?

Impossible.

Should she confess what she'd been trying to do to Bryn?

That was even more impossible—besides, there was no
need. She hadn't changed anything yet.

Should she talk Claire out of her marriage?

Oh, yeah, great! That way Bryn would hate her, Colin
would hate her, Joe would think she was an interfering
busybody…even Grandpa would say she didn't have the
right. She didn't *know* Claire was unhappy with Colin—
she just suspected.

There's no need to do anything, she told herself bleakly.
Colin may well decide not to change the wedding to the
chapel, and even if he does—well, it's his choice.

And Claire's choice?

Claire would have no choice at all, Sophie thought—and
that was the sticking point to the whole thing. But there
was nothing she could do about that. Some things were just
too hard…

She returned to the resort late that afternoon as there was
an evening wedding to prepare. It was a simple affair—the
bride and groom were marrying on the beach and they
wanted only the one posy—so she made up a simple bouquet of misty blue statice and roses. Finished, but still miserable, she walked down to the beach to watch the wedding.

This wedding couldn't be more different from the
McInerney affair. There were only six guests and no atten-
dants; the bride wore a simple gown which floated softly

to the sand, her feet were bare, her long blonde hair hung free and she looked up into her new husband's face with adoration. The adoration was returned in full.

Sophie stood on the water's edge, back from the wedding party, and she felt a lump rise in her throat as she watched.

'Penny for them.'

Sophie jumped about a foot. When she came back to land, Bryn was at her elbow, and her guilt and misery were flooding back in force.

'I…I beg your pardon?'

'Penny for your thoughts,' he said calmly, and watched her.

'How…how long have you been here?'

'I've been watching from the palm fringe,' he told her. 'This couple didn't want any hotel presence at all, but I like someone being around, in case…'

'In case the bride's father falls over drunk again?' Why was it hard to get her voice to work?

'That's right.' Bryn looked out over the small wedding party at the water's edge. The sun was almost set and a golden hue was lighting the evening sky as the last rays of the sun slipped behind the mountains. The waves were running in and out on the soft sand and the groom was helping his lady sign the register. Pan pipes were playing a melody Sophie hardly knew—hauntingly lovely and strangely familiar—as if it was an echo from an age past.

'I doubt there'll be drunks tonight,' Bryn said softly. 'This is lovely.'

'It's as it should be,' she agreed.

'Your flowers are gorgeous.'

'Don't tell anyone or I'll be out of a job,' Sophie begged. 'The posy's so simple it took me a whole ten minutes.'

'Sometimes simple's best.'

Silence. There seemed little else to say. She stood by

Bryn's side as the celebrant brought the wedding to a close, then the piper burst into something triumphant and the party made their way slowly—reluctantly, it seemed—up the beach and back to the hotel.

There was no point in staying longer—So go, she told herself fiercely—but it took a huge effort to make her feet move. She turned towards the track and Bryn fell in beside her.

Go away, she wanted to say, but the words wouldn't come. She was so muddled that her mind couldn't form one sensible idea.

'You wouldn't like to have coffee before you go home?' Bryn probed.

'I…no.' There was nothing for it but bluntness. If she tried to say anything more then she'd be stammering like an idiot.

'Because of Rick?'

'Yes!' Let him think that if he liked. Rick would have kittens if he knew, but it gave her some defence and Rick was half a world away.

'Lucky Rick.'

Sophie thought of Rick, up to his ears in coffins and everlasting daisies, and she couldn't suppress a smile.

'Yeah. He is lucky.' She kicked up a few palm fronds from in front of her on the track and thought of where she was compared to where Rick was. 'So am I.'

'He makes you smile?' Bryn was watching her with a curious look on his face.

'Yes.' Damn, why was her voice defensive? 'He does.'

'I wonder he can let you go for a whole month.'

'Believe me, he didn't want to.' Her smile grew a little wider. Poor Rick. 'But both of us can't leave, and he understands I need to spend time with my family.'

That was the end of that conversation. Bryn thought of

the absent Rick, and he could almost feel his teeth grinding. Damn him. What did Rick have that was so special? He strode on and Sophie had to skip a few paces to keep up with him. His frustration was mounting, and it showed.

'Where did you learn to speak Chinese?' he asked at last.

'In China. I travelled a lot before I settled down...with Rick.'

Bryn's teeth ground some more. 'Do you know any other languages?' His voice was strained.

'Some Japanese, French, German and some Italian,' she told him. 'But I certainly wouldn't call myself fluent, and I can't read or write in anything other than English.'

'That's six languages.' Bryn shook his head in bewilderment. 'That's some florist!'

'And you're some businessman.' She hesitated then, desperately unsure what to say. She was trying to hurt this man. She was trying to steal his wedding. And soon, tomorrow or the day after, Colin might telephone and change his wedding plans and Bryn would find out what she'd been doing. If she had to say anything, she should say it now, before the warmth in his eyes turned to contempt.

'I...maybe I shouldn't say this, but I think you're a special person, Bryn Jasper,' she whispered suddenly, and she stood on her tiptoes and kissed him lightly on the lips— then pulled away fast, before he could react. 'Last night was wonderful, and if I didn't have Rick, I'd be tempted to fall in love with you, right here and now.'

She took a deep, steadying breath, searching for the right thing to say as he stared down at her in the moonlight.

'But I do have Rick,' she whispered. 'So it's either throw a bucket of cold water over myself, or I need to take myself home right now.'

That was all she could say. She turned and fled down

the track without another word, leaving Bryn staring after her as stunned as he'd ever been in his life before.

'Claire Lleyton's been on the phone and wants you to ring her back.' Grandpa met her as she walked in the door, and he didn't seem to notice her flushed face. 'She sounds upset.'

Now what? Sophie desperately needed some time out, but she forced herself to phone Claire immediately. Had Claire found the courage to call off the wedding?

She hadn't, but she was distressed enough. 'Sophie, we're not changing the wedding arrangements,' she told her. 'We can't use the chapel. Colin rang Daddy in Paris and Daddy forbids it. Colin's angry but Daddy's paying, and Daddy says we're marrying at the resort.'

Sophie's breath came out in a rush and she leaned on the wall to give her strength. 'Thank you, God,' she said over and over, under her breath. She'd wanted Grandpa to have his Millennium wedding, but her deception had made her feel like a queen rat. Jane Bond wasn't her style. 'I've tried and I've failed,' she whispered. 'I can't do any more, and I don't have to betray Bryn.'

But Claire was sobbing on the end of the phone, and somehow she had to pull herself together to comfort her.

'Hey, Claire, it's okay.'

'It's not okay. I didn't realise how much I wanted a chapel wedding until I walked there with Joe this morning. It brought it all back—how much I loved the place and how much I loved you guys.'

'But you love Colin.'

'Y…yes.' Claire hiccupped and fell silent.

She had to do it. Bryn might still hate her if she put a stop to this wedding but it had to be said. 'Claire, are you sure you want to marry Colin?' Sophie asked. 'You know, it's not too late to change your mind.'

'Of course I want to.'

'Would you like me to come over?' Sophie paused, searching for the right words, and managed a chuckle. 'Even if I don't talk you out of marriage, I can share a drink. We can eat pizza and whinge about the men in our lives, and I'm good at sharing pre-wedding nerves. I can get them by watching a wedding from two hundred paces, so pity help me if I ever end up at the altar.'

Somehow Claire managed an answering chuckle, but her voice was still laced with tears when she replied.

'Thanks, Sophie, but I'm fine by myself. Leave me be. I'm just fine.'

CHAPTER SEVEN

THERE were no weddings now for another three days—thank heaven! Sophie badly wanted breathing space. It was as if now the deception element had been taken away from her relationship with Bryn she felt even more nervous. She crept into the resort every morning and did her arrangements with lightning speed, then spent her time working in her grandfather's garden, walking on the beach, talking with Grandpa—and jumping every time the telephone rang.

'You're nervy as a rabbit,' her grandfather told her. 'What's got into you, girl?' He looked at her intently. 'You're not in love, are you? There's not some man back in New York you're waiting to hear from?'

'N...no.'

'Not this Rick?'

'Not Rick, Grandpa,' she said, and managed a smile. 'Definitely not Rick.'

So what was happening? Bryn must know she was in the resort each morning, but it was as if he was having the same nerves she was having or had lost interest. Either way he was leaving her alone. By the third afternoon she'd decided the whole affair was ridiculous—and then he phoned.

'Hey, it's okay, Sophie,' John said, frowning as he handed her the phone. 'It's only Bryn.'

Only Bryn... Sophie lifted the receiver with fingers that shook, but the voice echoing down the line was cheerful and businesslike, as if there was nothing between them at all.

'Sophie, are you busy? I need you.'

Yeah, she needed him, too. Sophie clenched the receiver with fingers that were white with tension.

'Sophie, are you still there?'

'I'm still here.' Try to keep your voice normal, she told herself—and failed completely.

'There's an unexpected photo shoot on here.' Bryn sighed down the telephone. He hadn't noticed the tension in her voice but he obviously had other things to think of. 'You know the publication.' He named one of the big American glossy magazines, and she blinked in recognition. Wow!

'They've been up to Cape Tribulation to do a fashion shoot,' he continued. 'Fashion meets wilderness—that sort of thing. The trouble is, they hadn't done their homework. They wanted water shots, and the sea's full of stingers and box jellyfish; there's no stinger nets up there and the rivers are full of crocodiles. Their insurance doesn't cover them for models being eaten by crocs, so they've turned up here.'

'Yeah?'

'Yeah,' he said grimly. 'It was lucky I had room to accommodate them, and it's great publicity for the resort. I told them I had the room, but only if they gave this place prominent photo space.' He paused. 'You know the kind of thing. *The lovely Kirsty and the fabulous Marigold wearing next to nothing at the Marlin Bluff Resort...* So now, dearest, kindest Sophie...'

'What do you want?' She swallowed, and her voice came out sounding extremely suspicious, as if he was about to ask her to walk into a death trap.

'You sound like you suspect me of wanting *you* to wear next to nothing,' he complained. 'Which...come to think of it...'

'Bryn!' She could hear the smile in his voice.

'I want our florist to do the flowers,' he told her, and the smile was still there. 'I want *Flowers By Marlin Bluff Resort*—or even *Flowers by Sophie Connell of Marlin Bluff Resort* to be in the credits. I want my brides to know they can get everything here.'

'Bryn...'

'Now, I've just talked to your grandfather,' Bryn said. 'He does his hospital visits in Port Douglas on Fridays, so you're free all day tomorrow, and he doesn't have any sausages that desperately need eating. If you could come over now...sort things out... I need you tonight and tomorrow. Please, Sophie...'

Drat the man. *Please?* The man only had to say the word and she was jelly. She shouldn't go near him. Joe was right with his warnings, but...

He'd said please.

'Okay,' she said, and the word sounded feeble even to her. 'I'll be there in half an hour.'

'Good girl!'

Patronising toad!

Sophie put the phone down and tried to scowl, but it didn't come off. She tried hard to think miserable, but that didn't work either. She was off to do the flowers for a fashion shoot for one of the world's best-known magazines, and she was off to spend two days in the presence of Bryn Jasper—and she wasn't going to betray him after all.

Hey, anything was possible now.

The resort was humming.

Sophie walked into the foyer and stopped dead in astonishment. Before today the resort had been muted, giving off the sounds of hushed luxury and calm. Now the foyer was bustling with groups of photographers, editorial staff and clusters of long-legged models. There were piles of cameras and baggage scattered throughout, and the bellboys were running themselves ragged.

She stared around her in bemusement, but she wasn't left alone long. Bryn excused himself from a group of editorial staff and made a bee-line straight for her.

'Sophie…' He said the word as if he was clutching a lifeline, and she had to grin.

'Bad, huh?'

'They want floating islands of flowers,' he said desperately, almost clutching his hair. 'Tropical, colourful and floating! How the hell…?'

'Was that what they were trying to do off Cape Tribulation?' she asked, interested. 'No wonder they had crocodiles coming for miles. Do they have their own florist?'

'They have an artistic designer or some such. His job is to give the unfortunate resort florist orders. Another reason they left Cape Tribulation was that the poor florist up there wasn't up to the job. They're flying in their own flowers, and they've been saying they'll have to fly someone in from Cairns to do them. That was before I suggested…insisted on you.'

'Who's the artistic…?'

But then she caught the eye of a man over the other side of the foyer. He was six foot six or so, built like a string bean, bald, tanned and pushing fifty, and Sophie knew him well.

'Miles,' she squealed, and launched herself into the crowd. She flew straight through the piles of baggage as if they didn't exist, and right into the arms of her friend. Bryn was left to follow.

'I gather you two know each other?' he asked dryly as Sophie emerged from Miles's embrace, and Miles grinned happily across at him.

'Do I know Sophie?' Miles ruffled her close-cropped curls. 'Do I what! Sophie, what on earth are you doing here? Did I know you were working in Australia? No.' He answered his own question. 'I'm sure no one's told me that. Have you and Rick split up, then?'

'I'm just visiting my grandpa and helping Mr Jasper out of a jam.'

'Well, Mr Jasper, you have some help!' Miles put a long arm around her shoulders, hugged her hard again and turned to address Bryn. 'Why didn't you tell us it was Sophie you wanted us to use? There would have been no question. Sophie's the best florist in New York, bar none. If Rick didn't allow her to hide her light under a bushel, or stick it all on coffins…'

'Miles, that's enough,' she said crossly. 'Do I take it you're the artistic director giving poor Bryn all these head-aches?'

'We're paying "poor Bryn" handsomely for his head-aches.' Miles grinned cheerfully at Bryn. 'Originality equals headaches. But now I have Sophie… Islands is what I want, Sophie, love. Tiny islands just big enough for one model to lie on. I took one look at these fantastic swimming pools your Mr Jasper has, and that's what it has to be. Can we stick platforms out there and cover them with flowers to make them islands?' He frowned. 'I don't know, though. Platforms are immovable, and we'll have problems with the light…'

'How about if we do it with air beds?' Sophie said promptly. 'Hey, I knew my funeral work would come in handy some day.'

'Your what?' Bryn was floundering here, way out of his depth. 'Sophie, if you're thinking everlasting daisies…'

She chuckled. 'Nope, but close.' She spread her hands. 'Miles, I did the Fortingue funeral using everlasting daisies.

I couldn't get access to the coffin until an hour before the ceremony so I made the whole thing like a giant webbed sock, weaving flowers into the webbing, pulling it on the coffin at the last minute and then stitching it closed. If we did that using tropical flowers, and then filled our sock with an air bed...'

'I'd be able to take shots wherever I wanted,' Miles said, triumphant. 'Pull my islands into position wherever. Hey, Sophie...I could use three or four. Bring models together. Take shots into the sun and with the sea as background...'

'But they want to start shooting tonight,' Bryn warned, thinking it through. 'We're running short of time.'

'Then what am I hanging about here for? Miles, if you're supplying flowers and they're available now, then I'll have one island for you in an hour and a half, and another one in three. Two more by eleven tomorrow morning.'

'Sophie, you're an angel,' Miles told her, kissing her soundly on the forehead. 'And a genius. I don't know how you persuaded her to work for you, Mr Jasper, but you're a very lucky man.'

'I know,' Bryn said slowly, and he turned away as his attention was called for elsewhere.

I know, he repeated to himself slowly as he moved back across the foyer. Just not as lucky as someone in New York called Rick.

For the next three hours Sophie and Louise put their heads down and worked as they'd never worked in their lives. So did Miles and a couple of his assistants. Their work paid off. As the moon slowly rose in the east, Sophie watched the launch of her 'islands'.

They were truly gorgeous—a mass of exquisite cream-gold frangipani, soft blue hydrangea and white oriental lilies. The models were lifted, oh, so carefully, onto their beds of flowers so that the outside blooms wouldn't crush. As each shot was taken, any crushed blooms that showed were quickly replaced with others.

'Tomorrow we'll go bolder,' Miles said happily. 'There are red and yellow gerberas, blue iris, purple anemone, yellow freesias, white Singapore orchid, green cymbidium orchids and andomeda being flown in from Brisbane. The helicopter was taking them to Cape Tribulation but I've diverted it here.'

'Whew,' Sophie said, looking out to where the photographers were arranging the models on and around her islands. What this must have cost, first and last…

But it was magic. This was about as far a cry as it was possible to get from her funerals in New York. Sophie thought of Rick with his everlasting daisies and his sleet and his snow and his garbage strikes, and she almost chuckled out loud. This was florist heaven!

Then her heart missed a beat as Bryn came up behind her and placed an arm around her waist.

'Happy?'

Was she happy? Her heart started up again, but it was now racing way too fast. If she had to answer that question right now… Standing in the circle of Bryn's arm, moonlight on her face and the smell of frangipani and the sound of the sea all around her, she'd have to say she had never been happier.

'You smell of frangipani and all sorts of lovely things,' Bryn said softly, and he kissed her hair.

Sophie tingled from the toes up.

'Stay and have dinner with me,' Bryn murmured, and he must have felt her rising tension. 'The magazine staff are working flat out. No one here will have time to eat more than a sandwich on the run, but you and I are now free…

'N…no.' Heavens, how hard it was to say that word.

'Why not? Because of Rick?'

'Maybe.'

'Surely Rick couldn't object to you having dinner with your employer—or are you scared of what might happen if you have dinner with me?' His arm pulled her closer, so she could feel the warmth and strength of his body through the soft cotton of her overall. 'I'm not the big bad wolf,' he murmured. 'I don't eat maidens.'

'In my fairy tales, that reads pigs—not maidens,' she retorted, and managed to haul herself from his grasp.

'How about *Red Riding Hood*?' He grinned, and that grin was almost her undoing. He could ask for the world with that grin. 'Surely Little Red was a maiden?'

'Then where's the woodcutter with his axe when I need him?' she managed. 'Bryn, no.'

'You're prevaricating, Sophie. Why won't you have dinner with me?'

Why indeed? Because she was dead scared of falling in love with this man, she acknowledged. She was in danger of losing her heart in a big way, and there was no way Bryn was in the market for a long-term relationship. He'd made that clear.

'I...I promised I'd ring Rick tonight,' she said desperately. It was the truth. She was aching to know how his coffin-covering was going, but...she wasn't aching to know how Rick's coffin was going as much as she was aching to spend the evening with Bryn.

He sighed. 'I see.'

He didn't see at all. If he saw what was really in her head, he'd have her in bed in a flash!

'I'm—I'm going home,' she stammered. 'I'm not needed here and I need to be back early in the morning to do two more islands.'

'I'll walk you home.'

'No.' Sophie glanced at her watch. 'I... Joe goes for his walk at nine. I'll go with him.'

'You'd rather go with Joe than with me?'

She hauled herself up to her full five feet seven inches and tried a glare.

'I trust Joe,' she said bluntly.

'And you don't trust me?'

'No, Mr Jasper, I don't.'

He looked at her for a long moment, then his dark eyes creased into a self-mocking smile. 'You're probably wise,' he admitted. 'Just at this minute I don't trust myself. Okay, Sophie, go and find Joe and my dogs, walk yourself home and telephone your Rick.' He glowered. 'I just hope he's worth it.'

Sophie thought of Rick, and she couldn't suppress a rueful smile. Oh, heck... If Rick knew what she was implying about him...

'He thinks he is.' She deliberately made herself smile. Bryn mustn't suspect how she felt here, so...try for humour. 'And that's important in a man,' she added.

'You're saying your Rick has an ego problem?'

'Oh, not as big as yours.' Her smile widened. 'Ego's a male thing, Mr Jasper. I learned that long ago.'

'Sophie...' Bryn glowered at her, baffled. 'Has anyone ever told you that giving cheek to your boss isn't exactly the wisest thing for an employee to do? It's called insubordination.'

She twinkled. 'I know. You must have guessed by now that, apart from flowers and tricky clients, insubordination is what I'm chiefly good at.'

He didn't know how to respond to her. He shoved his hands deep into his pants pockets and stared at Sophie in the moonlight. She was so lovely, and so unattainable— and he wanted her so badly it was almost a physical pain.

'Stay tomorrow night,' he said bluntly, and watched her eyes widen.

'I beg your pardon?'

'There's a party on here tomorrow night,' he told her. 'The photo shoot will be over by then. The crew wasted so much time at Cape Tribulation that they can only stay two nights, so they fly out Saturday. They want a huge shindig here tomorrow to celebrate the end of their visit to Australia. It's poolside. Come.'

'Definitely come.' Miles appeared behind Sophie and placed a hand on her shoulder, adding to Bryn's pressure. 'No argument, Sophie Connell.' Miles looked down at her florist overall in frank disdain, his fashion sense offended. 'And make sure you dress up. I've seen how you can look when you try.'

He looked out at the long, leggy models scattered around the pool, a study in contrived beauty, and he grimaced. 'Show us what brains as well as beauty can do, Sophie, love. And come.'

She shouldn't go near this party in a million years. After a day working solidly keeping islands afloat, the next night Sophie went home to have dinner with Grandpa and to try to talk herself out of going back to the resort.

'There'll be so many people there they won't notice me,' she told John. 'I think I should get an early night.'

'They invited you?'

'Yes, but...'

'Sophie, you're not the least bit tired, and I am,' John Connell told her. He yawned. 'I know I should stop getting up at dawn and walking on the beach. It knocks me out at this end of the day and makes me lousy company.' He sighed. 'But I'll be leaving this place soon, and the dogs and I love it...'

Damn. Why was her heart twisting in so many directions? Sophie thought of John moving into Port Douglas to live with Ellie, and her heart twisted all over again. Grandpa loved Ellie and her family, but his heart was here, at his beloved Marlin Bluff.

She felt so helpless, yet there was nothing she could do. There was no way Sophie could outbid Bryn for the land, even if it was possible for John to stay on here by himself, and now she'd lost him his wedding…

Her unhappiness must have shown in her face. John leaned forward and placed his hand on hers, and he gave her a weary smile.

'Go to your party, Sophie, love,' he told her. 'Get on with your life. Don't let my sadness infect you. I've had a good life here. It's time for me to move on.'

Why can't Colin change his mind? Sophie thought desperately. It was the only thing that could cheer Grandpa up. A Millennium wedding…

But there was no way she could ring Colin and put more pressure on him; nor could she ring Claire's father. She'd tried sabotage once, and she'd failed, and there was no way now she could backstab Bryn. It was all just too hard.

'Sophie, go to your party,' Grandpa said again. 'Let an old man go to bed in peace.'

If she went to the party, then at least she wouldn't be lying staring at the dark and turning herself in circles, she thought bleakly.

She was mad to go.

She was going!

What to wear?

Something demure, her head said, but her heart didn't agree, and 'demure' wasn't in her wardrobe. Her hand drifted from hanger to hanger. She hadn't brought much in the way of evening wear, but her fingers moved instinctively to the turquoise silk, and there they rested. Dared she?

She'd found this dress in a Fifth Avenue window and loved it on sight, then walked back and forth past it about six times before trying it on. By the time she'd carried it back to work, she'd convinced herself she was crazy.

'So try it on,' Rick had insisted, and she had—and his eyes had almost popped out of his head.

The dress clung to her like a second skin. It was cut in an oriental style, with short sleeves, a high neckline and a pencil-slim skirt reaching just above her knees and slit down the side. The description sounded demure enough, but the dress was anything but demure!

The lovely material—shimmering turquoise silk—seemed almost translucent; the lining hid all it needed to hide, but in such a way that it appeared the lining was simply a trick of the light, or a shadow. If she moved a little differently then all could be revealed... The dress was respectable, but only just, and it certainly didn't look respectable at first glance.

Should she wear it? Was she brave enough—or stupid enough? Or both!

Her glossy black curls clung around her face, framing her pale skin. She did her eyes carefully, accentuating their size, then slipped on high, high stilettos—and then grimaced and slipped them off again. She could do without a broken ankle.

But...dared she go like this? Dared she wear this dress near Bryn?

She was wearing it for Miles, she told herself, but she didn't believe it for a minute.

Okay. Let's go, Sophie, she told herself. And go fast, before you turn chicken and run. She took one last, long look in the mirror, and stuck her tongue out at her reflection. This was crazy. The party should be in full swing by now, and among all Miles's gorgeous models she'd be unnoticed.

So get a hold on yourself, Sophie, she told herself crossly. You're not trying to compete with anyone for anything.

Except she was. She took a deep breath, closed her eyes, then took her stilettos in her hand and walked firmly outside, closing the door behind her.

Bryn Jasper, here I come!

A hundred yards along the beach, Bryn separated from the shadows among the palms—and it was all she could do not to turn and run. Why on earth did her heart stand still every time she saw the man? The way she was going she was heading for cardiac arrest!

'I thought you'd decided not to come,' he told her, as he strolled down the beach to meet her. The moon was casting a ribbon of light across the waves, lighting their path.

'Where's Joe?'

'He's taken the night off. He has urgent business, he told me, and he asks for so little time I could hardly refuse. He's hardly taken a day off since he started.'

'So…' It was hard to get her voice to work, or to keep her words from sounding breathless. 'So where are your dogs?'

'I couldn't hold your hand in the dark if I brought the dogs,' Bryn said soulfully. 'And I thought you might need hand-holding. Aren't you scared of the dark?'

'Not until now.'

'You could sound a little bit grateful that I've come to fetch you,' he complained, and Sophie relaxed a little and smiled.

'Fetching defenceless females… That sounds like you

intend to put me over your shoulder and carry me back to
your stronghold, ready or not.' Her voice was still breathless, but she hadn't broken pace. She kept walking steadily
towards the resort and let him fall in with her, and she
didn't let herself look up at him.

'Caveman-style,' he agreed. She heard laughter in his
voice as he walked on beside her. 'I've mislaid my club
but that's what I am—a caveman, claiming my own.'

'But of course I'm not.'

'Not?'

'I'm not your own.'

'That's right,' he said softly. 'You're Rick's.'

'I'm not anyone's!'

'But tonight…'

'Tonight I don't belong to anyone at all,' she said, and
her voice was tight with strain.

'Now that's just wonderful,' he said softly, and he took
her hand in the moonlight, brooking no argument. 'Let's
take it from there, shall we, Sophie Connell, and see what
happens? On a night like this—who knows?'

The party was well under way when they reached the resort.
And Bryn was too blatantly eligible to be permitted to be
monopolised by an unknown such as Sophie. There were
models of international repute here. Sophie was cautiously
eyed, and gently edged aside.

Bryn made a determined effort to hang onto her—especially when he finally saw the dress under the lights—but
Miles would have none of it.

'Sophie, you're gorgeous,' he roared over the noise of
the band. Miles looked her up and down, approving absolutely, and Sophie flushed crimson. 'I'm taking her to
dance,' he told Bryn.

'Hey, I walked all the way along the beach to find her,'

Bryn complained, his stunned eyes still on Sophie's dress, but Miles was having none of it.

'And very nice it was of you to fetch her for me,' Miles purred. 'Thank you very much, Mr Jasper.' He doffed an imaginary cap and swept Sophie out onto the dance floor.

The dance floor was a tiled area where the hotel grounds met the beach. The band was playing on a raised platform with the ocean as backdrop, and it was quite the most beautiful setting Sophie had ever danced on.

'So what does Bryn Jasper have that I don't?' Miles murmured into her ear as the band slowed down to a waltz and he pulled her in close. 'It poured with rain for the whole time we were in Cape Tribulation—and the *wind*! It was side effects of Hurricane Linda, or some such, so we come down here and your Mr Jasper snaps his fingers and the sun comes out...'

'He's not my Mr Jasper,' Sophie managed.

'Oh, yes, he is, darling,' Miles told her. 'Your face is in my neck, Sophie, love, or you'd see him, but from where I'm watching he's surrounded by four of the most gorgeous women in the world and yet he's watching you as if he'd like to put daggers into me.'

'Miles...'

'You've got him on a string,' Miles said, wonderingly. 'Now, what are you going to do with the poor man?'

'Nothing,' she crossly.

'Sophie, you can't make a man look at you like that and then not do anything with him.'

'If he ever found out what I've been trying to do with him, there'd be no decision to make,' Sophie said, and Miles stopped dancing and put her away from him at arm's length.

'Sophie, are you kidding me? You're not trying to cross him?'

'Only in business,' she said hastily, and Miles shook his head in disbelief.

'No!'

'Well…yes, but I didn't succeed.'

'Thank God for that.' Miles hauled her back into his arms and danced on. 'Cross Bryn in love and you might get away with it. Cross him in business… Well, I'm heading for the other side of the world tomorrow. If you succeeded, there'd be nothing for you to do but join me.'

CHAPTER EIGHT

ON ANY other night, Sophie would have enjoyed herself enormously. The setting was the best she could ever have imagined for a tropical party. The music rang out under the stars, the soft ocean breeze was warm and caressing, and the people here…well, they were just plain gorgeous. Or rather, they weren't plain at all, she thought as she looked around at the fabulous dresses on the even more fabulous supermodels!

The male and female models were so beautiful they were breathtaking, and every person here was out to soak up this last night of tropical warmth before heading back to the bleakness of New York's winter.

Despite the competition of the female models, Sophie wasn't left without a partner for a minute. Miles claimed her for dance after dance, but the magazine's editorial staff and the male models were right behind him.

It hardly mattered. All Sophie was interested in was Bryn, dancing with one gorgeous model after another, and by mid-evening she was so jealous she could have screamed.

How could she be jealous of the women in Bryn Jasper's arms? she demanded of herself.

Because she was madly, totally besotted with him, she told herself crossly, and to be besotted with Bryn Jasper was tantamount to being a complete dope. The man was a multimillionaire. He could snap his fingers and women would come running. She'd be lucky if he looked at her twice after she left this place—even if he never found out she'd been trying to double-cross him.

Bryn needed a florist; he was flirting with her a little and that was all there was to it, she told herself as she watched him dance. His kiss had meant nothing—apart from a little practice of his tried and true seduction technique—so Sophie drank another glass of champagne, smiled brightly at her latest partner and danced on into the night, while Bryn danced with whoever he liked.

Who he danced with was no business of hers.

But if she was confused and heartsick, so was he. Bryn danced with his beautiful models, but he watched Sophie. Dear God, she was lovely. That dress… The man she was dancing with pulled her closer, and Bryn found his hands clenching hard behind the back of his lovely partner.

His partner looked up at him—a leggy blonde with eyes that could drown a man's soul—and he hardly noticed.

'Is something wrong?' she asked brightly, and he sighed. This was stupid. He couldn't concentrate.

'I'm afraid you'll have to excuse me,' he told her, feeling not the slightest pang of guilt as the music paused and he made his escape. Such a lovely girl would be left partnerless for the whole of two seconds, if that. 'I need to see about the…about the catering.'

'Goodness,' she murmured. 'I didn't realise your job was so hands-on. I thought you'd employ a manager for that sort of thing.'

Bryn did, and Warwick was more than competent, but he wasn't going to admit it. Wondering at himself—a week ago he would have revelled in the company here tonight!—he smiled his apologies and made his escape.

First he went to the kitchen, where his chefs and his waiters needed not the least supervision of their catering, and then he wandered out to the beach, where he stood in the shadows and glowered at the dancing crowd. Or rather, at the dancing Sophie.

What on earth was eating him? he demanded of himself. He'd never felt this way about a woman. Maybe once he'd thought commitment was possible, but Tina's death and Elise's betrayal had taught him some pretty strong lessons. Hell, there was no way he could be ripped apart like that again, and the way he was starting to feel about Sophie was the way of madness.

'Sulking?' There was a glow in the dark behind him and Bryn swung around to find Miles watching him with detached interest. He hadn't seen Miles leave the dance floor, but then, he hadn't seen anyone other than Sophie.

'I just strolled down here to light up a cheroot, dear boy,' Miles told him. 'Litigation's gone so far I need a personal exhaust fan if I'm to smoke these days, and it doesn't do one's image much good to have a fan whirling over one's head like something in a comic book.'

Miles hauled his cheroot from his mouth and eyed it with contemplative stillness. He cast Bryn a thoughtful look and decided to go with smoking as a safe conversation topic for the moment. 'I'm taking a risk if I stand here and talk to you, dear boy,' he confided. 'If in forty years you get lung cancer, you won't sue?'

Bryn managed a smile. 'I promise. No litigation.'

'How about against the man dancing with Sophie?' Miles asked, his eyes still contemplative. 'Would you be just as charitable to him?'

'I beg your pardon?'

'I've been watching you, and you've been watching him.' Miles took a couple of deep draws on his beloved cheroot. 'Sophie and Edward make a handsome couple. Lovely girl, Sophie,' he said softly—and waited.

'Yes.'

'Edward could be forgiven for being enamoured…'

'He's not.'

Miles puffed on his cheroot, and watched Edward and Sophie for a while. 'Maybe not yet,' he agreed. 'After all, this is only Edward's second dance with the lady. But you?'

'Me?'

'Are you enamoured?'

'Don't be ridiculous.'

'No,' Miles agreed quickly, hearing anger flare. 'Of course not. Stupid idea, dear boy.'

Silence. The band played on, and out on the dance floor someone tapped Edward on the shoulder—but Edward shook his head and held Sophie closer. She turned laughing eyes up to him and Bryn practically ground his teeth. Miles watched in amused silence.

'You don't think you should ask her for a dance yourself?' he suggested. 'They're about to start their third dance, and after three dances anything's possible. I mean…it couldn't do any harm.'

'I don't…'

'You don't want to dance with her?'

'Dancing with other men's women,' Bryn said through clenched teeth, 'is not my style.'

Miles stilled. He looked out at the couple on the dance floor again and he frowned.

'To my knowledge,' he said carefully, 'Sophie has never met Edward until tonight, and this is only the start of their third dance.' He tapped his cheroot and puffed on. 'You know, as far as long-standing, inviolate relationships go, I wouldn't say this one tops the list.'

'Not Edward,' Bryn snapped. 'Rick.'

'Rick?'

'She won't have dinner with me because she has to

phone Rick,' Bryn muttered. 'She won't do anything because of Rick. You asked her yourself when you met her here yesterday. *"Have you and Rick split up, then?"* But they haven't, and she's going back to him. I've asked her to act as florist here as a favour, and I can hardly try to break up a partnership when I'm employing the girl.'

'Bryn, I think I admire your morals,' Miles said, and suddenly there was a choke of laughter in his voice. 'But I suspect Rick wouldn't thank you for them.'

'Why not?' Bryn turned away from the dancers and stared at Miles in the moonlight, his voice laced with strain. 'Hell, man, what do you mean?'

'Well, Rick's Sophie's partner, all right,' Miles said, and his words were a trifle unsteady. 'Rick owned the Fifth Avenue florist shop when he met Sophie, and offered her a partnership because of her talent, but he's exacting his pound of flesh from her. She's very much a junior partner, and she knows it.'

Miles eyed his cheroot for a while then, considering his words. He was deeply conscious of the sudden absolute stillness from the man beside him. 'When I asked if Sophie had split from Rick...well, I wouldn't have been surprised if she had broken from the partnership,' he said finally. 'Things have been pretty tense lately between the pair of them. People are asking for her, you see, and Rick doesn't like it...'

'But...' Bryn swung around again to stare across the dance floor at Sophie. 'But...by partners...you mean... business partners only?'

'Yes.'

'Sophie implied more.'

'Then she'll have her reasons for doing so, dear boy,' Miles said calmly. 'Rick's pushing fifty, pushing twenty stone, and, if Sophie was the least bit interested, his Josie and his three charming children might well have something to say about it—but, as I said, Sophie always has her reasons. Maybe you could ask yourself what they could be.'

But Bryn wasn't asking himself anything. He'd turned away and was striding across the beach to the dance floor, and if the look in his eyes meant anything at all, Miles thought reflectively, Edward wouldn't be dancing with Sophie for very much longer.

Two men had tried to interrupt Edward's dancing with Sophie while Bryn had been watching. Neither had succeeded. Edward's arms were holding her close, claiming her as his own.

Bryn wasn't as formal. He came from behind and simply lifted Edward bodily and placed him to one side. Before Edward could do so much as gasp, Bryn had Sophie in his arms and was whirling her to the other side of the dance floor.

'What the...?' Sophie was almost too surprised to speak. 'Hey, excuse me,' she managed. 'I was dancing with Edward.'

'*Was* is the operative word,' Bryn said silkily, and his hands held her around the waist, drawing her in so her breasts were crushed against him. 'You *were* dancing with Edward. Now you're dancing with me.'

'But I don't want to...'

'Don't want to dance?' Bryn's eyes glinted down at her, dark and fathomless in the dim light. 'No? Very wise, my lovely Sophie. I have something else in store for you.'

Before she could even make a squeak of protest, he'd swept her up in his arms and was striding off the dance floor and down to the beach, leaving his guests—models, editors and Miles—staring after them in astonishment.

'Bryn, put me down.'

It was a full thirty seconds before Sophie found her voice, and, when she did, they were a hundred yards from the dance floor and her voice came out a squeak. 'Bryn...'

'Why should I put you down?' His arms gripped tighter. 'The last thing I want is to put you down, Sophie Connell. You've been driving me crazy since the first time I saw you, and in that dress...' He groaned, not lessening his stride for a moment. 'You don't know what you do to me in that dress.'

She shouldn't have worn it, she thought numbly. She should have worn a nice little number in something like sackcloth.

'I...I was enjoying dancing with Edward,' she managed.

'I'm sure you were.'

'And I was enjoying dancing with Miles and Patrick and...'

'Sophie.'

'Yes?' She looked uncertainly up at him in the dark. Her arms were around his neck, but only to steady herself, she told herself desperately. It was only to stop herself falling— not because she really wanted to hold onto him any way she knew how....

'Shut up,' he said softly.

'But where are we going?'

'I'm looking for something.' They'd reached the beach by now, and Bryn was striding along the shoreline, searching the sand in the soft light cast by the moon and the resort lights above them.

'Wh...what?'

'Wait 'til I find it.' Then he saw what he was looking for. Holding her tightly against him, he scooped and gathered something in his hand before she could see what it was. Then he set her on her feet, holding her so firmly she couldn't wriggle free. Brooking no protest, he calmly lifted

her dress forward from her throat—and let one blob of jellyfish slither down her neck and into her bra.

Sophie squealed.

'You…you…'

'I know.' He grinned. 'I'm sorry. It was a very unchi-
valrous thing to do. Childish, really. I can't think where I
got the idea from. But now we've exchanged jellyfish…
What greater token of devotion can a man give?'

'Bryn…' She was trying hard not to choke on laughter,
and desperately fumbling to loosen her bra, but the dress
fitted too perfectly. She needed to take it off, but…

'Can I help?'

'Get away from me.' She backed away. 'Of all the crazy,
deceitful…'

'Sort of like implying you and Rick were an item?'

'We are.'

'With Josie and the three kids?' he agreed.

'I hope Miles chokes on his cheroots,' Sophie said
through gritted teeth, hauling her bra futilely away from
her. She whirled and stalked off down the beach, umbrage
seething from her rigid back. 'I'm going home,' she flung
over her shoulder.

He caught her in two seconds flat, whirling her up and
holding her in his arms again. 'Nope.'

'What do you mean, nope?'

'By the time you get home, the jellyfish might have
given you a rash,' he said softly. His eyes glimmered down
at her in the moonlight. 'I know they're harmless, but
there's no saying how some people react.'

'They don't give me a rash.'

'They might, and then I'd feel guilty. You wouldn't want
that to happen—now would you?' His eyes fixed hers. He
stood motionless on the warm sand while she lay in his
arms and tried to think of something—anything—to say.

For the life of her she couldn't think of a thing to say—
or do. Somewhere down her bra she had a jellyfish, and
she should be thinking about it, but she wasn't. The feel of
the jellyfish was forgotten. Suddenly all she was aware of
was the feel of Bryn's arms around her and the look of
tenderness in his eyes. Everything else was forgotten. This
had gone past laughter—past any point she'd ever crossed
before.

'Rash,' he said softly, and she knew he was reading her
thoughts. 'We need to concentrate on the rash.'

'Wh…What do you suggest we do about it?'

'My apartment is just beyond the rise,' he suggested. 'I
could take you there and help you…'

'You mean take off my dress?'

'If that's what it takes.'

She stared up at him, her eyes troubled, but he looked
calmly back down at her in the moonlight and all she could
see was tenderness.

'Why did you lie about Rick, Sophie?' he asked, in a
gentle, loving voice that was her undoing.

'Because I was afraid,' she said simply.

'Afraid?'

The time for pretence was past. The night was deep and
dark and wonderful, and somehow there was only room for
the truth between them. 'I've never felt about anyone in
my life before as I feel about you,' she told him simply,
and her clear grey eyes shone with honesty. 'It scares me
stupid, Bryn, and I don't know what to do with it.'

Silence. The silence went on and on. Their gazes re-
mained locked, and in that long moment something passed
between them that was akin to a wedding vow. Bryn set
Sophie on her feet and took her hands in his.

Sophie was shaking. Her whole body was trembling.

Bryn put his arms on her shoulders and the touch made her shudder. He swore very softly and drew her into him.

'Sophie, what is this?' He held her against his heart. 'There's no need to be afraid. Hell, I won't hurt you,' he promised. 'I'll never hurt you. I swear...'

'I didn't think you would. I don't...'

'Then what?' He held her away from him and stared down at her in the moonlight with eyes that were troubled. 'What, my love?'

'I don't...' She shook her head, trying to clear the fog. There were so many unanswered questions. Bryn was so rich and so powerful. Could there be any future for her in such a man's life? Was there any future in the way he looked at her?

Who knew? But for now she loved this man. She knew this now with a clarity that had her at a loss to know how she'd been so blind until this moment. This wasn't lust or infatuation—with her whole heart and her whole being she loved him.

And if she did—surely it wasn't wrong to take this night, and accept the emptiness of tomorrow...tomorrow?

Sophie took a deep breath. She looked up at her love— her Bryn—and she smiled. The shaking stopped. For once...for now...Sophie was sure.

'I love you, Bryn Jasper,' she whispered. 'I love you and it scares me to death, but there it is. I love you with my whole heart, as I've loved no other.'

And he could do with that as he pleased. Independent career woman? Ha!

Once more there was silence, but then Bryn sighed, softly in the warm night air, and his sigh told Sophie that he'd just been given a gift of unbelievable value. She wasn't stupid to have said such a thing. She wasn't!

'My love,' he said softly, and he gathered her closer

against his heart. 'My love,' he said again, and his words were like a vow against her hair. 'My heart.'

And then he was striding up the beach with his treasure in his arms, kissing her as he went, tasting, holding, wanting... There was no room for words—no room for anything but sensation. The night was exploding around them, and there was nothing else in the world but what lay between them.

Whatever the morning would bring, for this moment there was only Bryn and Sophie... One.

The morning came too soon.

Sophie stirred languidly in her lover's arms and looked over his shoulder through the window. Somehow through the night they'd ended up in Bryn's vast bed, and the wide French windows beside them looked right down to the sea.

There was still no rain, Sophie thought dreamily. This was heaven. It was the rainy season, but the rain had taken time out.

Bryn felt her stir, and his arms tightened, but she pulled away, touching him lightly on the lips.

'Wait...'

His eyes flew open. 'Wait for what?'

'You'll see,' she teased him. 'But first I have obligations, even if you don't.' She laid a finger on his lips, silently asking him to hush, and she lifted the telephone on the bedside table.

'Sophie...' Grandpa answered on the first ring. 'Where are you, girl? I've just come back from my walk and I was about to bring you a cup of tea.' She could sense him staring at her bedroom door, puzzled.

'I stayed at the resort.' Sophie's voice faltered as she searched for an acceptable explanation. 'The party went on late, Grandpa, so the resort staff gave me a bed.'

'You're okay?'

'I'm fine—just a bit too tired to walk home.' Oh, help. Sophie was stark naked as she perched on the bedside and talked—and Bryn had silently started to stroke along the long line of her spine... Concentrate!

'I have an eleven o'clock wedding, so I need to start doing the flowers now,' she told her grandfather. That much was the truth. 'I'll come home about lunchtime.'

'Sophie... You sound...different.'

She was! Any minute now she'd lean back and let her lover have his wicked way with her. The way his eyes gleamed laughter...and his hands...!

'I'm fine, Grandpa.'

'Bryn's looking after you?'

'He is.' Now how on earth had she managed to say that without laughter in her voice?

'Then don't you worry about rushing home on my account,' John told her. 'Take your time. Enjoy yourself.'

'I will, Grandpa. I just need to do the flowers for this wedding...

'And I *do* need to do the flowers for this wedding,' she told her love as she replaced the receiver. Both his hands were holding her now. He was kneeling on the bed behind her, his arms cradling her back against his chest, and it was all she could do to speak. Her body was burning with want. 'Bryn, there are wedding f-flowers...' she stammered. 'The wedding's at eleven. I need to go.'

'Liar,' he said softly into her hair. 'You can do the flowers in a flash.'

'My bride wants a trailing bouquet of lisianthus, roses, berries, ivy, asparagus fern and mini-gum,' Sophie said, trying for asperity—and failing dismally. 'If you think I can arrange that in a flash...'

'I know you can.' His mouth was moving from her hair,

down the nape of her neck and then lower, leaving a trail of kisses as he went. 'You can do it in your sleep, and you're sleeping with me. Now! So no problem…'

'You call this sleeping?' She felt light and hot and dizzy, and altogether too wonderful for words. She arched herself back, then twisted to place her hands on his face and kiss his wonderful mouth—and he kissed her right back. She could drown in his kiss…

'If our bride complains about her flowers this morning, then I forgive you,' Bryn said magnanimously. 'I won't dock any more than fifty per cent of your wages.'

'Gee, thanks.'

'I'll make it up to you in other ways.'

'Such as?'

'Services rendered,' he said promptly, rolling back with her onto the bed. 'I'll do anything you like, only tell me what, dearest, sweetest Sophie. Tell me how I can serve you.'

'Well…' Sophie's eyes raked her lover and her eyes flared. He was magnificent! 'I *can* think of something.'

'What?' Both of them knew exactly what she was thinking. Her eyes said it all.

'How about making me a cup of tea?'

That set him back. He gave a shout of laughter and then pulled her in close.

'Really? A cup of tea?'

'Absolutely, sir,' she said primly, and her arms encircled his wonderful body. 'In about twenty minutes, I want a cup of tea—or maybe a bit longer…maybe a lot longer!'

CHAPTER NINE

SOMEHOW Sophie pulled herself together enough to do the flowers for the Barkley wedding. In fact, they *were* tricky, and she was forced to concentrate. Rhiannon Barkley was a fashion designer who knew exactly what she wanted, and it had to be right.

It was. She could have done anything this morning, she thought happily as she surveyed her finished bouquet. She could conquer the world this morning. The bouquet was beautiful and the bride would look truly lovely carrying this.

Louise watched Sophie out of the corner of her eye as they worked.

'You look different,' she said softly.

Sophie grinned her cat-got-the-cream grin. In fact, she did look different. She was wearing jogging pants and a loose T-shirt that said 'WIMBLEDON LAWN TENNIS 97'. It was not her style, but she'd hardly had a choice.

'Did you go to Wimbledon?' Louise asked, and Sophie had the grace to blush.

'Well, no. This belongs to a friend.'

It belonged, in fact, to Bryn's mother. She would have looked really stupid turning up to work this morning in turquoise silk with bits of jellyfish attached, Sophie thought ruefully, and the alternative would have been to beetle back along the track to the chapel wearing a towel. Luckily Bryn's mother seemed about her size—'and she always leaves half her gear behind when she visits,' he'd told her.

'She'd even have left her goldfish if the dogs hadn't eaten them. There's no way she'll mind you wearing these.'

Despite his assurance, Sophie had put the clothes on with mixed feelings. Maybe these belonged to Bryn's mother—or maybe they belonged to one of his former girlfriends. Frankly, though, in her current state of euphoria, Sophie didn't care. What was past was past, she decided, and Bryn was her future. She started on the bridesmaid's posy and she hummed as she worked.

'It's good to see you happy, at least,' Louise told her, and Sophie glanced up at the tone of her voice.

'Why? Is someone unhappy?'

'Joe.'

'Yeah?'

'Haven't you noticed?' Louise demanded. 'He's down-right miserable. He brought those palm fronds in just now and he hardly said a word.'

Sophie hadn't noticed, but then she wasn't really noticing anything. She forced herself to think about it now. Joe *had* seemed quiet.

'Maybe Bryn's dogs have given him distemper,' Sophie said darkly. 'They'd give me distemper—or at the very least a migraine.'

'He loves the dogs.'

'Then what?'

'Beats me.' Louise shrugged. 'Maybe he's crossed in love, though I didn't know he had a girlfriend. He's so self-conscious about his scar that he never asks anyone out.' She looked more closely at Sophie and gave a maternal smile, as if she guessed the source of Sophie's happiness. 'Next time you see him, see if you can share a little of your sunshine. It seems you have more than enough this morning.'

She was absolutely right, Sophie thought. She had happiness to spare. She finished her wedding arrangements, fixed her foyer centrepiece, and then, on impulse, walked over to the wedding centre to watch Rhiannon's wedding.

It was a lovely, simple service. The bride looked stunning, dressed in deepest burgundy. The groom wore a deep black morning suit and top hat, his only colour a burgundy buttonhole. Against the black and burgundy, Sophie's pink and purple bouquet looked fantastic. Sophie watched until the end, and as the 'Trumpet Voluntary' sounded, and bride and groom turned to face their guests as man and wife, she found her eyes welling with tears. She turned away—to find Bryn watching her. He grinned and handed her a handkerchief.

'Don't tell me,' he teased gently. 'You always cry at weddings.'

'No. Yes!' She looked up at him and gave a defiant sniff. Luckily they were out of earshot of the wedding guests, hidden discreetly behind service screens. 'Go away.'

'Nope. I came to find you.'

'Wh…why?'

'Because I figured you'd have finished your flowers.'

'So?'

'So I can take you back to bed,' he said cheerfully. 'Unless you have any objection, my love?'

Sophie looked up at him from behind her handkerchief— and she couldn't think of a single objection.

They were halcyon days. The days flew, and Bryn seemed in as great a state of wonder as Sophie.

'I never thought I'd find a woman like you,' he told her. 'Even now I can't believe it. Something will happen and this will fade to a dream.'

No! But Sophie looked into his face and found herself worrying. She must be imagining it, she told herself, but it was almost as if there was a trace of fear in his eyes. She loved him, and held him against her, but there was a tension about him she didn't understand. Still, he made love to her as if she was the most desirable creature on earth, and surely that was all that mattered?

This wasn't fantasy, she told herself dreamily over and over. It wasn't! And she must be imagining Bryn's tension. She was in love for ever.

For ever lasted until Saturday.

Saturday morning was always frantic at the resort. Saturday to Saturday was standard time for most people's holidays, and arrivals and departures were always three times that of other days. Sophie turned up at nine and made her way through a crowded foyer. Bryn wasn't around. Well, that was to be expected.

There were no weddings, so Louise had the day off. Sophie intended to spend the morning doing an arrangement for the foyer, and then…maybe meet Bryn for lunch?

She checked her watch and made a silent bet with herself. She'd never been in the florist's workshop for more than twenty minutes before Bryn had found an excuse to come. How long now?

It wasn't twenty minutes. It was five, and his face said it all. The fantasy was over.

Sophie looked up as he entered, and her heart almost stopped. She'd never seen him look like this. His face was as rigid as if it was carved in stone, and his eyes were freezing.

'H…hi,' she managed.

'Why are you still here?' His voice was as cold as his look. He came two feet into the room and stopped, as if coming nearer would contaminate him.

He might look cold to Sophie, but that was how he felt,

he told himself bleakly—cold to the bone. For Bryn, his fantasy had ended. It had been a crazy soap bubble, he told himself harshly, and now it had burst. He'd tried to give away a part of himself that he'd held in storage for years, and he'd got what he deserved.

'I... Bryn, what's wrong?' Sophie stammered.

'You've got what you came to get,' he said coldly. 'There's no reason for you to stay.'

'But...why?'

'I've just had a phone call from Daniel Lleyton, Claire's father.' Bryn stared across at her as if he couldn't figure her out and he shook his head. 'Do you realise what you've done?' he demanded softly. 'Do you know how much this will cost me?'

'I don't...'

'Don't come the innocent with me,' he snapped. 'Daniel's in France, but he says you've been working on Colin to change the wedding venue. Daniel was opposed to the change, but it seems his wife thinks it's romantic—and she's persuaded him to change. The wedding's now to take place in the chapel.'

'But...'

'I've invested a fortune in this, and you think you can interfere... It'll cost me...'

That got to her. Slowly Sophie rose to her feet, her eyes not leaving her face. Emotions kept tumbling through her head and she couldn't figure out what was most important. There was so much at stake here—but he was angry about money!

She couldn't know that his anger at money hid a deeper anger—and a deeper hurt.

'Cost you?'

'Yes. Cost me.' His eyes flashed scorn. 'This is the biggest thing... I have photographers coming from all over the world for the Millennium celebrations. In many cases I've paid for their travel and accommodation, because the publicity will be fantastic. Because of the time lapse we're half a day in front of the US and Britain. There's time for them to write their copy and have Millennium photographs on the front pages of their papers on the first of January. We could get coverage on every major tabloid in the world.'

'And…you need Claire and Colin…'

'The wedding's only part of what we've planned, but it's huge. I've brought photographers here with the promise that there'll be a wedding. What the hell am I supposed to say now? That I lied?'

'You can say the bride and groom changed their mind,' Sophie said with asperity. 'It's their prerogative.'

'Only they didn't change their mind, did they?' he said silkily. 'You changed their minds for them.' He moved then, stalking over to grip her shoulders, and his grip was like a vice. 'Is that why you came here, Sophie? To steal this wedding? If so, why the hell did you end up in bed with me? What nasty little reason did you have for that?'

Sophie closed her eyes for one long moment. He sounded as if he hated her, and there was nothing for her to give him but the truth. She owed him that, at least. If only he could understand…

'I did come to take the wedding,' she whispered. 'At first that's what I intended, and I wanted it more when I realised that Claire wants to be married by Grandpa, but Claire's father said they wouldn't change and I was relieved. Despite Claire's disappointment, I thought…I thought it was over. And as for the rest…Bryn, I love you.'

She wasn't reaching him. He let his hands fall from her shoulders, took a step back and stared.

'Why?' It was one flat word, devoid of emotion, but it was hanging between them, demanding an answer.

'Why do I love you?' Sophie could hardly speak.

'Don't be stupid.' His voice was deliberately cruel, driving her away. Love couldn't come into this, his words said. This was business. 'Why did you sabotage this wedding?'

'I didn't think I had!' It was a wail of distress, but it still didn't move him.

'You have, and I want to know why.'

'Because it's Grandpa's Millennium wedding!' she managed, trying desperately to make him see. 'Grandpa's done so many weddings. In the old days—when I was little— the chapel was booked out months ahead. Grandpa sometimes did two or three weddings a week, and he loved them. This one should have been his two thousandth wedding, on the first day of the Millennium, and his last before he retires.'

'You mean you took this job so you could slime your way…'

'I didn't slime my way anywhere. Claire wants to be married in the chapel.'

'You're promising them free flowers and publicity?'

'Yes.' There was no denying that.

'They can get better publicity here.'

'Then tell them that,' Sophie flung at him. 'But, Bryn, Grandpa wants this wedding so badly! He won't admit it, but he does, and so does Claire. If you talk them out of it now…'

'It's my business, Sophie,' Bryn said flatly. 'I'm a businessman.'

'And I'm a businesswoman,' she retorted. 'But I know where my heart lies, and it doesn't lie with money.'

'So where does your heart lie, Sophie?' he demanded, his voice lowering to dangerously quiet.

There was only one answer to that. There could be only one answer—while Bryn was watching her as if she'd committed the worst crime known to man. She'd cost him money.

'On this, my heart's with Grandpa and Claire,' she whispered softly, and only she knew the tearing of her heart as she said it. 'If Claire didn't want to be married in the chapel then it would be different, but she does. I'm sorry, Bryn, but that's the way it is.'

Silence, and in that silence Sophie died a little. When Bryn finally spoke, she already knew what he was going to say.

'Get out of my hotel, Sophie. Get out now.'

'I'm leaving.'

It could never have worked, anyway. That was the gist of what Sophie told herself for the next two days, but it didn't make her feel better. She'd never felt more miserable in her life.

At least Grandpa was happy. John wandered around humming the 'Wedding March' and practising sermons on the dogs, and his smile didn't leave his face. Claire had come herself to ask if he'd marry her, and John couldn't have been more pleased.

'She's such a nice child,' he told Sophie. 'If only I could be happier about her young man.'

'Her parents approve.'

'Do they, Sophie?' John said, his smile slipping a little. 'I would have liked it better if he'd come with Claire. They must be certain this is right.'

'Now don't you go sabotaging our wedding,' Ellie told him crossly. 'You know darn well it's what Claire wants. Sophie's gone to a huge amount of trouble to get it for you, and it's going ahead now even if I have to get behind bride and groom with a shotgun.'

The Millennium wedding in her sights, Ellie bossed them

all. She had them polishing, painting, scrubbing…and everyone who came near the chapel was roped in to help. So, with the laughter and bustle, it was possible for Sophie to at least shove her unhappiness onto the back-burner and hide it from the others.

'It'll be the best wedding,' Joe said in satisfaction. There was no way he was supporting Bryn in this. He was backing Sophie all the way—plus he was supporting Claire. Claire spent her days working around the church; she radiated her happiness that her wedding would now be in the chapel, and Joe spent all his spare time helping—and watching her.

Joe was destined to be more involved. 'I want you to play your bagpipes,' Claire announced when John asked about music, and Joe stared.

'You're kidding.'

'No. You played the bagpipes at school and I know you still can.' Claire gave him a shy smile. 'I think you sound fantastic.'

'But…'

'And if I find you a true Highland outfit, will you wear a kilt? Please?' She stood on tiptoes and kissed him. 'Please, Joe…'

'But…what about Colin…your parents…?'

'They're not here to make the arrangements so they can lump it,' she told him, for once firm in her decision. 'You in your kilt is what I want. Will you do it?'

He couldn't refuse. Joe couldn't refuse her anything, Sophie thought. He nodded helplessly and Claire smiled, then her fingers reached out and touched his face, tracing the scar running down its length. It was a touch of thanks, but Sophie saw the shudder of his long frame and flinched. Oh, heck…

Joe was in for as much pain as she was.

*   *   *

Joe drove Claire home late that afternoon, and then went back to work. Ellie went home, Grandpa went to bed, the Labradors settled to sleep, but Sophie worked on, polishing the brass fittings of the church as if her life depended on it. She was going quietly nuts!

Joe found her there, and one look at his face told her that she wasn't the only one going quietly crazy—he was desperately unhappy too—but then he told her why he'd come and things became immeasurably worse.

'The wedding's changed,' he said flatly. 'It's at the resort again.'

Sophie's polishing hand stilled. She rose to her feet and stared at him in silence, and her face lost its colour. 'What do you mean?' she asked at last.

'Bryn's offered them a free wedding. He rang Daniel Lleyton in Paris and gave him a list of everyone who'll be here. And he's showed the list to Colin.' Joe groaned. 'Hell, Sophie, you never really thought you'd get away with it? Bryn has rock stars and actors and even minor royalty coming.'

'But…Claire doesn't want that.'

'No.' Joe was practically speechless with rage. 'She doesn't. She rang me just now, and she's been sobbing her heart out, but there's no way she'll stand up to bullies like Colin or her father…'

'Or Bryn…'

'Sophie, Bryn's a businessman.'

'Yeah, but to do this….' She paused as the enormity of what he'd done sank home. Dear God… Bryn was just as bad as any of them, she thought savagely, riding roughshod to get his profit.

'Claire's coming to see John tomorrow to tell him,' Joe told her. 'She was too upset tonight, but…I thought I should warn you.'

'Thank you,' she said slowly, and walked to the door.

'Where are you going?' But there was no need to ask. He could read it in her face.

'You do what Claire wants,' Joe shouted after her as she broke into a run. 'For God's sake, Sophie, that girl's had enough. Between the pair of you, you're making her life hell.'

Yeah! That made her feel just terrific!

Bryn was doing slow laps of the pool. To stand on the edge and yell would just about choke her, so she sat in the shadows and waited, anger building by the minute. John's smile and Claire's laughter played over and over in her mind, and by the time he'd finished swimming she felt physically ill.

Finally he emerged, grabbed a towel and made his way toward his apartment, and Sophie stepped out of the shadows to greet him.

'Sophie…' He took a step back and his face closed in the moonlight. 'What do you want?'

All the way here and all the time she'd spent waiting she'd been rehearsing what she'd say, but now, suddenly, it was all too much. Sophie's rage was threatening to consume her. This man, his money and his power, could crush people like Claire and John between his fingers and not even notice. She closed her eyes—fought for control—and she lost. Her hand came up and she slapped a ringing, stinging slap right across his cheek.

Then she burst into tears.

'You toad,' she managed through sobs. 'You conniving, rotten *toad*…'

'Sophie…' Bryn caught her arm but she wrenched it away in fury.

'Don't you *Sophie* me. You…'

'Toad?' Damn, he was laughing at her, and there was

triumph in his laugh. 'Hey, Sophie, isn't this a bit melo-dramatic? We've had a business competition here—and I've won.'

That was all it was, Sophie thought furiously. He'd won. Well, he hadn't been so calm when he'd lost, and he'd only lost money!

'You—you don't have a clue, do you?' she stammered. 'Not one clue. It's all business to you. All you care for is money and power and prestige…'

'What else is there?'

What else indeed? Sophie took a step back and stared up at him, but there was nothing on his face but blank incomprehension. He was looking at her as if he didn't understand a word of what she was saying—or thinking.

Dear heaven, could she really have imagined herself in love with this man? She must have been mad!

'There's Claire,' she said savagely. 'Claire wants to get married at the chapel, but you don't give a damn about that, do you?'

'She's one half of the wedding,' Bryn said flatly. 'Colin wants the wedding here, and if she doesn't want it then it's up to her to disagree.'

'As if she would…'

'I've hardly met the girl. How can I—?'

'And then there's my grandfather,' she interrupted, as if she hadn't heard him, and somehow she forced her voice to be calm. 'Bryn, Grandpa came to Marlin Bluff thirty years ago. It was a large community then, and he expected to stay a few years and move on. Like you, he was ambitious.'

'What's this got—?'

'Shut up,' she said icily. 'Shut up, Bryn Jasper. You're going to hear this if I have to get a megaphone and shout it from the rooftop of your damned resort.'

'I…'

'So my parents were killed in a car crash,' Sophie said, talking into the night as if she was talking to herself. 'Grandpa was a widower—a man alone—with plans to move up the church's hierarchy. But after the crash he told the church he wasn't interested in promotion. Unlike you, Bryn Jasper, he decided there was something more important than money and blind ambition.'

'I don't…'

'He settled down and he made the best of his life,' Sophie went on. Damn Bryn; he'd done so much damage the least he could do was listen. *'The best,'* she repeated. 'He gave Ellie and me the most loving childhood two children could ever have, and he gave the community of Marlin Bluff the *best* care. He married them and he buried them and he cared for everyone here like he cared for his own. Nothing was too much trouble.'

'This doesn't…'

'But then Marlin Bluff changed,' Sophie said bitterly. 'The population moved away. Still, he was happy with his tiny congregation, but then even that disappeared. Bryn Jasper and his damned Marlin Bluff Resort took over. Sure, the residents were happy to move into Port Douglas, but what was left here for Grandpa?'

'Sophie, he's retiring anyway…'

'Oh, sure,' She spread her hands. 'He is, and there's not even a congregation left to say goodbye to him—except there's one girl, a girl called Claire, who really wants him to marry her and who thinks, like me, that for him to perform the Millennium wedding would be something special.'

Silence. There was absolute, total stillness. Even the frogs, raucous on these hot, still nights, were silent, each taking in the enormity of what Sophie was saying.

Only it wasn't enormous, Sophie thought sadly. It wasn't

even important. It was just one old man's sadness and one
girl's helplessness. What could that matter? She still wasn't
looking at Bryn. She was looking down at her linked
hands—trying so hard to get the words out without breaking.

'When Claire asked Grandpa to marry them,' Sophie said
softly, 'Grandpa was *so* pleased. It wasn't like a congre-
gational farewell, but it was almost as good. It's his two
thousandth wedding on the first of January on the year 2000
and his last wedding before he retires.'

She did look at him then. Sophie stared up through the
dim light into Bryn's blank face and she tilted her chin.

'But money and ambition and power don't take into account an old man's joy,' she said softly, 'or a young girl's
wishes. You and Colin, your bank accounts, your world
press and your blinding ambition…you don't give a damn.'
She took a deep breath.

'Sure, I came here to interfere with your plans,' she told
him. 'But I did it from my heart. Believe it or not, sometimes all money is good for is destroying something so
precious it can never be replaced.'

'Sophie…'

'I want nothing for all the floristry work I've done for
you,' she managed. 'It'd choke me to be paid. I've wanted
nothing but Grandpa's joy. And when I made love to you,
it was because I thought I loved you. But you… Maybe it's
you who should be marrying the obnoxious Colin, because
you sure as heck deserve each other.'

And then, with a choking sob, and before he could say
a word, she turned and fled into the night.

CHAPTER TEN

BRYN spent the night wide awake.

After Sophie had left, he'd spent a long time staring down the darkened track after her. Should he have followed? He didn't know. There was a kaleidoscope of impressions fighting for space in his mind and he couldn't work them out.

There were two major images fighting for supremacy.

One was a girl who'd accepted a job within his organisation solely to get what she wanted—to damage his plans and to pull his Millennium wedding into disarray.

Had she smiled at him because she'd needed to be charming to betray him? Had she made love to him so she could achieve her ends? God knew. Bryn didn't any more. A girl who could accept a job so she could betray her employer and get what she wanted was capable of anything.

In a way, Bryn understood that. He hadn't built a hotel chain by being a nice guy, and there had been times when he'd questioned his own morals, but he'd never done anything like this—and if he hadn't been so emotionally involved he might have guessed what she was up to.

Regardless, he'd turned the tables. Bryn tried to make himself smile at the way he'd swayed Colin and Daniel Lleyton to move the wedding back to the resort. That list of fame and royalty had been the clincher. Bryn knew exactly how to manipulate power-hungry little weeds for his own ends, and Sophie would just have to lump it.

All's fair in love and business...

But…for Sophie it wasn't business, and there was John Connell and Claire mixed up in this. The little people…

Here, then, was the second image—Sophie lying in the mud and laughing up at his dogs, Sophie watching weddings with tears in her eyes, and the memory of her lying in his arms…

He couldn't trust her, he told himself fiercely. He'd expected the joy to end, and it had!

There was no way he'd sleep tonight. Bryn dressed, then, on impulse, collected Marty and Goggle from their run and walked down along the beach to the chapel. There was a light burning in the house. Sophie?

'She used me,' he told the dogs, trying to keep his anger burning—but it didn't work, and the dogs put their heads to one side and looked at him as if they didn't believe him either.

'All's fair in business.'

Nope, they didn't believe that either. Marty put a wet paw up on his knee and looked at him soulfully, as if he understood. This wasn't business for Sophie, Marty's big eyes told him. This was love—love for an old man, whose needs Bryn hadn't even noticed, and for Claire, whose wants he hadn't considered.

'Hey, how could I have noticed their needs? I'm a businessman. If I want this resort to be a success then I can't let emotions sway my judgement.'

His emotions were swaying him now, and the dogs looked as if they knew it. They whimpered against his hand as he stared up the beach at Sophie's home. 'It's okay, guys. I'm not going dotty here,' he told them—but was he? He closed his eyes and an image appeared—not the lovely, laughing Sophie he thought he'd fallen in love with, but the Sophie flashing fire, and with tears welling behind her eyes.

'I did it from my heart,' she'd said, and he knew, in his own heart, that she had.

But that was *his* heart talking—not his head. So much was at stake that he must use his head now. So many influential people were coming from half a world away to be present for this Millennium wedding that if he made the wrong decision then the future of the whole resort would be in jeopardy.

But…Sophie?

'I can't trust myself,' he told the dogs. How could he? His crazy hope—that here was a woman with whom he could spend the rest of his life—had been twisted and distorted until he no longer believed what his heart was telling him.

It was all just too hard, he thought bleakly.

The light in Sophie's bedroom flicked off and the house fell into darkness. Bryn stared at the darkened window for a long time—his dogs standing sentinel—and then slowly he turned away and the trio made their way back to the resort.

He didn't take the dogs back to their run. They spent the night on his bed, and God knew he was grateful for their company. Wearily he forced himself to concentrate on Millennium plans as his dogs snored gently into the night. He couldn't let himself think of Sophie. He mustn't! But there were matters pressing on his conscience as heavily as the dogs were pressing on his legs, and they were matters that couldn't give him rest.

It was late before Sophie surfaced the next morning. She'd lain awake and stared sightlessly into the dark all night, consumed with misery and heartache, and she hadn't fallen asleep until after John had left for his morning walk with the Labradors.

She vaguely heard his return, then heard the phone ring and John's quiet words of comfort—that would be Claire, sobbing her heart out on the end of the line. John replaced the receiver and knocked on her door.

'Awake, my Sophie?'

It was the term he'd used for her since she was two years old. *My Sophie.* Damn, she'd cried herself to sleep and now there were tears welling the minute she opened her eyes.

'Oh, Grandpa,' she whispered, and John walked in and took her into his arms, just as he'd comforted her when she'd stubbed her toe, or had a fight with her first boyfriend.

'You know, then.'

'Joe told me last night.'

'Hey, Sophie, you're not to take this to heart,' he said softly. 'It's Claire's wedding, and she's to have it where she wants.'

'You know she wants it here.'

'I know she wants to keep her fiancé and her father happy—so we'll support her every way we know how,' John said sternly.

'But it was to be your celebration.'

'Then let's celebrate another way. We can have a picnic on the beach the night of the Millennium, to mark my retirement.'

They would too, she thought sadly, and it would be good—sort of. They'd have a family celebration, then watch the fireworks and listen to the music from the resort that would soon take over this whole headland.

Damn Bryn! But she managed a shaky smile, and squeezed John's hand—then paused at the sound of a knock on the outer door, followed by fierce barking.

'That'll be Joe with Bryn's dogs,' she told John. 'He was pretty upset last night.'

Ellie and Sophie had been trained since childhood to

close their ears whenever John's parishioners came with problems, so, as John answered the door, she deliberately tuned out the rumble of male voices. Not that she could have heard anything anyway—Marty and Goggle had been locked outside and were in full voice.

Today she'd book her flight back to New York, she decided bleakly. She'd set her return for January the fourth or fifth. That would give her time to help Grandpa move into Ellie's home, and say goodbye to this place as it was handed over to Bryn.

How could you have given your heart to such a rat? she asked herself desperately. I thought you had more brains, Sophie Connell. You know how many women have fallen over themselves for Bryn Jasper, and now you're just another name on his list of conquests.

She felt angry and humiliated—and desolate.

Anger! That was the emotion to centre on here. She could cope with anger. It was the desolation that bit the deepest.

Furiously she threw off her bedsheet, padded through to the bathroom, and spent ten minutes standing under cold water, trying to feed the anger and wash the desolation away.

'Sophie…'

The bathroom door opened a crack, just enough to let John speak to her.

'Grandpa?'

'Bryn's here,' Grandpa said softly. 'He wants to talk to you.'

'Bryn!'

'That's right.'

She took a deep breath. What on earth…? There was only one response, though. 'I don't want to talk to him.'

'I'd prefer that you did,' John said apologetically. 'And soon. His dogs are destroying my garden.'

'His dogs…' Sophie stuck her head out from under the water. 'It was Bryn who brought the dogs?'

'Yes.'

'He's been here all this time? I thought it was Joe.'

'It was Bryn. He wanted to speak to me and now he needs to speak to you.'

'But I don't want to speak to him!'

'Sophie!' John's voice grew uncharacteristically stern. 'I need you to talk to Bryn while I've still got a garden left. Now.'

'But I'm wet,' Sophie wailed.

'Then dry yourself.'

'Grandpa, I can't. I don't want to.'

'I think you do,' John told her softly. 'We're waiting for you, Sophie, love. Come out and hear what Bryn has to say.'

It took five minutes to towel herself dry, run a comb through her hair and throw on shorts and T-shirt, and by the time she had, she felt as if she'd run a marathon. She was so hot! She put her palms up to her burning cheeks and fought back the colour. How could she face him? What could he possibly have to say?

She walked through to the kitchen in bare feet, with no make-up and wet hair. Bryn was sitting at the kitchen table, a mug of tea in front of him. He rose when he saw her, but she slipped into a chair at the other side of the table, putting as much distance as possible between them.

'Grandpa says you want to see me.' Her voice was flat and expressionless, and she stared straight down at the table. Dear God, she felt ill. She couldn't look at him without wanting him, yet she'd tried to deceive him and now he was being a rat. Everything was crowding in on her, and the only thought that was constant was the knowledge that she loved him! Despite everything, despite knowing she was a king-sized twit to feel as she did—she loved him.

'I do.'

'I don't know why you should.' Then Sophie broke off as Bryn's dogs started howling outside. The cacophony was truly awful.

'Why on earth have you brought the dogs?' she demanded. That, at least, was a safe subject.

'Joe's away and they're bored stupid.' Bryn put a hand up and raked his fingers through his dark hair. He looked weary to the point of exhaustion. 'All this and my chief groundsman takes a sickie.'

'A sickie?' Sophie's eyes widened in concern and she finally looked up at him. 'Is there something wrong with Joe?'

'I don't know. I just know he rang in this morning and said he wasn't fit to come to work. The man's been looking haggard for the last few days. I assume it's the flu.'

Or something else, Sophie thought. Joe hadn't looked as if he had the flu when she'd seen him last night—he'd looked as if there had been something deeper wrong.

She didn't say anything, though. John poured her tea and she took her mug and cradled it between her hands, as if taking comfort from the warmth.

'What do you…?'

The dogs started barking again and John rose. 'I feel a walk on the beach coming on,' he said.

'I don't blame you.' Sophie winced. 'With this noise…'

'I'll take Bryn's dogs with me.' John smiled from Sophie to Bryn and back again. 'You two need to talk.'

'No, we don't.'

'Yes, you do.' John gathered his granddaughter's hands between his and fixed her with a look. 'Bryn has just made me an offer—an extraordinary offer that means I need a walk to take it in. I want you to listen, Sophie, love, and soak in every word, because I hardly can. And now I'm off to walk the dogs and clear my head—and you're to sit here and listen.'

She could hardly refuse, so Sophie sat motionless, staring down at the table as she listened to her grandfather quiet the dogs. John was good with dogs. His own Labradors were old; they were used to comings and goings, and they now lay peacefully under the table, supremely uninterested in what was going on, but once they'd been boisterous pups and John had trained them well. It hadn't been Grandpa who'd fed them licorice allsorts.

'Sit,' she heard him say sternly, and there was sudden blessed silence. 'Now, if you two act like gentlemen, then we'll get along very nicely. No, I said, sit, sir. Very good. Now, at a nice, docile walk, let's go. Lead on...'

Bryn's jaw dropped. 'Now why the hell...? They never do that for me.'

'Grandpa has a way with dogs.' Sophie stooped under the table and gave her own Lily a pat. 'Hasn't he, girl?'

Lily looked up with adoring eyes, uttered a gentle woof and went quietly back to sleep. These dogs had had their own early-morning walk, and this was time for serious siesta.

Even Bryn fell silent.

'I...I'm sorry I hit you last night,' Sophie said stiffly, fighting for something to say. That was one thing she regretted—to actually slap someone...

'I forgive you.' Was she hearing things—or was there laughter back in his voice?

'That's big of you.'

'Magnanimous,' he said gently. 'As is my wont.'

'Oh, really?'

'Really. Sophie, will you come back and do my flowers? I have a bride tomorrow who's changed her mind at the last minute and wants daffodils. Can you tell me where we'll get daffodils in Australia in December?'

'You won't,' she told him. 'And we...*you*...won't be able to fly them in from overseas by tomorrow.'

'But you'll be able to persuade my bride to change her mind, won't you, dearest Sophie? Negotiation is what you're chiefly good at.'

'No.' She was watching his face with doubt. He was playing a game here she didn't understand. 'I've told you, insubordination is what I'm chiefly good at.'

'That's okay. I've discovered I can cope with a little insubordination.'

'What I did,' Sophie said carefully, 'is a lot of insubordination. And you...'

'I know. I insubordinated right back.' He grinned. 'I'm a master of the art. Underhand weasling is my art form, as making mud angels is yours.'

Sophie gasped and stared. Good grief! How dared he sit there on the other side of her grandfather's table and laugh at her!

'Sophie...' Bryn saw the look of anger wash across her face and he reached out to take her hand. She snatched her fingers back as if his touch burned. 'Listen.'

'I...'

'Sophie, I have a plan.'

'I don't need to hear it.'

'Yes, you do. Sophie, last night you told me to shut up and listen, and I did. I listened, and it made me see some things very clearly. So now it's your turn.'

'But...'

'Sophie, I've bought this house. I've bought the chapel and I've bought all this headland. It was due up for auction next month, but you must have known I intended buying. I thought by waiting for the auction I could get it cheaper, but this morning I rang the church authorities and offered them a ridiculously high figure if I could get immediate possession.'

'Immediate…'

Sophie's face went deathly white. 'But…'

'I need immediate possession if I'm to have my plan working for the Millennium,' he told her. 'We only have a couple of weeks, with Christmas in between, where nothing gets done. I want an army of workmen starting work now.'

'Bryn…' Sophie shoved herself to her feet and took a blind step backward. 'You mean…you want us out? Now? Today?'

'No.' Bryn didn't move from where he was sitting. He was watching her face. 'That's just it, Sophie, I don't. Under my plan, John—and you too if you like—can stay for as long as you like. Indeed, I hope John does stay. I need him.'

It was too much. Colour was washing in and out of Sophie's face and she put her fingers up as if to feel her face was still really there.

'I don't understand.'

'I've been a bit blind,' Bryn said apologetically. 'In fact, I've been very blind. When I built my resort, this church wasn't for sale. Therefore I ignored it and I built the biggest, most beautiful resort possible, including a wedding centre. When the church was advertised, I didn't think laterally. I thought—what else do we need?—yep, we need an aquatic centre, and this headland is a good place for it. I've been travelling so much I never really stopped to look at it, and I was too stupid to see that this could make Marlin Bluff more special than any resort in the world.'

Sophie shook her head, confused. Her eyes were fixed on Bryn. 'I still…'

'So I lay awake all last night, thinking,' Bryn said. 'Then this morning I walked over to our wedding centre and looked at it—*really* looked at it—and I saw a wonderful place to hold a reception, but I didn't see a magic place to hold a wedding.'

'It's lovely.'

'But it's not special,' he said gently. 'That's why I have many brides who marry on the beach or in the mountains or…' He spread his hands on the table. 'Or lots of places. They only use the resort for the reception. Maybe they still will. The beach is still lovely, but it rains, and there are people who want an inside wedding, and there are people— many people—who want a church wedding.'

'So…' Sophie's hands had stilled. She was standing hard against the wall, seeking support from its strength—otherwise she might well fall over. She was afraid to breathe.

'So some time about dawn I walked over, and I looked for a long time at this little chapel standing on the headland, where it's stood for a hundred years, and I went inside and I saw what you were saying last night—that my money was destroying something so precious it could never be replaced.'

'So what…what are you going to do about it?' Sophie's voice was blank and expressionless, but her heart felt as if it was standing still—forgetting to beat. A tiny thread of joy was forming somewhere in the back of her head and filtering downward…

'What I've done.'

'Which is?'

'As I said…' Bryn's voice matched hers for lack of emotion but his eyes never left her face. 'I've bought the chapel, and now I've talked to your grandfather. I've offered him residence here and a salary until such time as he wants to retire, and then we can come to some arrangement about him remaining in this house. I've asked if he has any objection to doing inter-denominational weddings—if he'll marry whoever wishes to marry in his chapel.'

'But…he always has,' Sophie whispered. 'He's always believed it was his privilege to bless a couple in marriage. So…' The thread was becoming a warm and wonderful mass, flooding her body and threatening to overwhelm her, and she could hardly take in what he was saying. 'So he will?'

'He will. If he likes he can still run his weekly services here as well, and…'

'He doesn't have to retire,' Sophie breathed. 'He doesn't have to move. Oh, Bryn…'

'And he can do our Millennium wedding.' Bryn smiled. 'We'll improve the track between the resort and here—all the land now is mine—and we'll have the wedding to end all weddings. We'll have the ceremony here and the reception at the resort, with bridal arches all the way along the track.' Bryn's eyes were flashing, and Sophie saw the businessman in him surface again. 'It'll be magic. You'll see.' He looked up at her, and his face was suddenly uncertain. 'What do you think?'

What did she think? Sophie wasn't sure whether to laugh or cry. If Bryn had stood…if he'd risen and taken one step towards her, then she would have tumbled into his arms— but he didn't. He stayed sitting at the table, his hands resting before him, and there was suddenly a weird restraint between them.

If either of them made a move now, then the move would be permanent. Vows hung in the air, and they were to be made for ever, but there was enough uncertainty on his face for her to know that this wasn't just about his Millennium plans. His uncertainty lay in his feelings, and his willingness to embrace the vows she'd already made.

'I'm… Bryn, I'm sorry for what I said last night,' she stammered

'Don't be,' he said, and there was a strange note of formality in his voice. 'It needed saying.' Then he hesitated, and the tension grew worse. 'There are so many things to get under way… I need to get back.' He rose, but didn't come towards her—not one inch. 'Will you come back to work to do the flowers?'

What, now? With him? By the look on his face, Sophie didn't think so.

'Come back?' she whispered.

Bryn hesitated. Come back, was what he desperately wanted to say. Come back to my arms.

But he'd expected Sophie's betrayal. He'd known all along that this love business was fantasy, and he was damned if he was opening himself to hurt yet again.

'We need a florist,' he heard himself say. 'I can't run a Millennium wedding without you.'

He needed her only for business. Of course. What else was there? Sophie swallowed. So… So what? What was she hoping for, here? A miracle?

She knew what she was hoping—for the love in her heart to be returned in full—but it seemed that it wasn't about to happen. The closeness, the passion and the love that they'd shared such a short time before now seemed a thing of the past. Was it over for ever? Had she killed it?

Or…had it never really existed in the first place? Was Bryn simply moving on? He'd bedded Sophie, so maybe that was enough. Was it time for him to move on to the next of his women—his next conquest? He still needed her as a florist, but nothing more.

Sophie wiped her palms on the sides of her shorts. She

couldn't complain, she told herself desperately, but inside she felt cold and sick. She'd as much as thrown herself at him, so she had only herself to blame for how she felt now.

Her feelings couldn't matter. There was no choice now but to do what he was asking. He'd thrown her grandfather a lifeline and now he needed her, but he only needed her flowers and she had to accept.

'Of course I'll come,' she said stiffly. 'And, Bryn...thank you for what you've done for Grandpa.'

'My pleasure,' he told her. He stood and looked at her for a long moment, as if drinking in his fill of her, and then he turned and walked out through the door.

CHAPTER ELEVEN

BRYN didn't just leave Sophie—he left Australia. He barked orders right and left and then headed for France. He was needed there, he informed his manager, but he'd be back for the Millennium.

And Sophie...

Sophie should have been happy, she told herself over and over. After all, she had what she'd come for. Grandpa was joyful and Claire seemed delighted at the outcome, though she seemed quieter than her normal bouncy self. Ellie's shriek when she heard the news had practically ruptured her eardrums, and everything Sophie had hoped to achieve by coming home from New York had been achieved with bells on. Even Joe managed a smile when he appeared back at work.

'It's great news,' he told Sophie. 'My men will make the track between here and the chapel a picture. We'll do your grandfather proud.'

'That's great,' Sophie told him. She was arranging a Christmas wreath, but she laid aside the berries she was working on and turned to face him, putting her own unhappiness aside. He still had shadows. 'Joe, are you okay?'

'Sure,' he said, but his assurance was just a little too fast. 'There's nothing wrong with me.'

'You were ill.'

'Flu or something.' He shrugged his shoulders. 'It made me really depressed and I had to get away from the place for a bit to find space to breathe. It was my first day off since I started work here eighteen months ago, so Bryn didn't mind.'

'But…are you still depressed?'

Joe chewed his bottom lip and looked steadily at Sophie.

'No more than you, I reckon,' he said slowly. 'You've got shadows under your eyes, too. Do you reckon we've got the same strain of flu?'

She closed her eyes. Was it so obvious? When she opened them Joe was still watching her, and his eyes were kind. It was true. They wore the same shadows, and if he felt as she did…

'Is it Claire?' she whispered, and he nodded.

'What do you think?' he said bitterly. 'Of course it's Claire.'

'You love her?'

'Anyone would.'

That was what she thought about Bryn, and if Joe felt as she did… 'Oh, Joe.' She sighed. 'Have you told her?'

'Oh, yeah!' Joe swore and turned to face out of the window to the mountains beyond. It was raining outside, steady, steaming rain as if it was raining tears. 'Yeah, I'd tell her, wouldn't I? Hey, Claire, I know you're marrying Colin next week but what about looking me over first? I'm such a great bargain—a man with a limp and a face that'd scare kids…'

'It doesn't scare kids, and you'd make a lovely husband, Joe.'

'As a husband, I make a great dog-walker,' Joe said bitterly. 'No. For God's sake, Sophie, she's marrying Colin. There's no room in her life for me. I'm not about to make her feel sorry for me by telling her.'

'But…'

'Look, it's useless,' Joe said, and his tone said the topic was closed. 'I've agreed to play the bagpipes at her damned wedding and that's enough. But what about you? At least Bryn doesn't have another woman.'

'Joe…'

'You can't tell me you're not in love,' he said softly. 'I've watched you and I know you well enough. You're eating your heart out.'

'Hey, Joe…' She sighed again, picked up her berries and absently started to pick them from the stem. 'You and I are just a couple of kids from Marlin Bluff,' she said softly. 'What would the great Bryn Jasper want with the likes of me?'

'The man's a fool.'

'He can have any woman he wants.' She tried hard to keep her voice light—and failed. 'Why would he just want the one?'

'Hell, Sophie…'

'It is, isn't it?' she said bleakly. 'It's just hell.'

Christmas.

The time for joy.

Sophie had spent the last five Christmases overseas, so Ellie was determined to make the most of her sister's homecoming. With so much to celebrate, there seemed no reason why the whole world shouldn't be happy.

So Sophie tried as hard as she possibly could, and Ellie was too busy to notice her preoccupation. Her grandfather did, but, even though John watched her, his wrinkled face creasing in perplexity at questions he couldn't answer, he didn't probe. Even if he had, Sophie wouldn't have been able to tell him. After all, there was nothing to tell, for her brief fling with Bryn Jasper was over.

Bryn found Christmas even more dreary. He'd made a fast trip to France, spent a few days checking things were run-

ning smoothly at La Ville, and then had decided to stay on
and spend Christmas with his mother.

She had been surprised, but agreeable. Marie had been
born a Frenchwoman, and her extended family lived around
and in the hotel. Since Bryn's father had died she'd become
more of a Frenchwoman than ever. Bryn's two uncles
worked with her as joint managers of La Ville, and Marie
was never alone, but having her son for Christmas was an
unexpected bonus.

'Is there something wrong, Bryn?' she probed on
Christmas night. He was flying out the next day—flying
back to oversee the final preparations for the Millennium
at Marlin Bluff.

'No. Why should there be anything wrong?'

'It's just...' Marie hesitated. She knew her son and knew
he hated probing, yet... 'It's unlike you to be so quiet.' She
laid a hand on his arm and looked up into his rigid face.
'Don't think I haven't enjoyed having you to myself this
Christmas, but every other time you've come you've either
dived straight into business with your uncles, or you've
come with...with a friend. But now...' She hesitated.
'Bryn, there *is* something wrong, no?'

'I don't...'

'Is it a woman?'

'No.'

'Bryn...'

And then the dam burst.

'Oh, of course it's a woman,' Bryn burst out. 'Hell and
damnation, Mama, of course it is.'

'But...'

'There are no buts.'

'Is she married?' Marie's heart sank. Her lovely son...
There had been so many women, and all of them had made
Marie cringe. They had been so elegant—so beautiful—and

all of them so aware of how they'd looked on her handsome son's arm.

'No.'

'Tell me, then. What is the problem?'

Bryn shoved his hands deep into his pockets and turned to face the fire. This was crazy! Christmas here meant snow and log fires. Christmas at home…

Home? Home should be here, he told himself bitterly, with his uncles and his mother…

'I'd make a hell of a husband,' he said.

Marie's face stilled. This was serious, then—very serious.

'Would I like her?'

'No. Yes. I don't know.' Bryn put his fingers up to rake his hair. 'How can I tell? She's like no one I've ever known. She mocks me. She tells me all I care for is money and prestige and power.' His fingers fell to touch his face, as if he could still feel the bruise where she'd slapped him. 'I don't know whether she loves me or whether she's just using me for her own ends. She betrayed me in business, she throws jellyfish at me rather than kiss me—and she hit me!'

A muscle twitched at the side of Marie's face. 'She's a businesswoman and…she hit you? She has a temper, then. She sounds like a Frenchwoman. I shall either hate her or I shall love her.'

'Mama…'

'I know.' Marie's smile died. 'So…my son, you are finally in love.'

'It won't last.'

'Are you sure of that?'

'Mama, since when has any woman ever interested me for more than a month? You know I can't love. Not…not like you and Papa. Not since Tina, and then Elise…'

'Bryn, Tina was your twin sister and you loved her very much,' Marie said softly. 'You were inseparable, but she's been dead these past ten years. Then you thought you were in love with Elise, but truthfully, Bryn, Elise was a Tina lookalike who had nothing to offer, and it was too soon after Tina's death for you to see. She was only after your money and you were lucky you realised in time. Since then, you've entered every affair with the expectation that it will end. You've learned not to trust, you've hardened your heart as a barrier against pain, but it's time it softened again, opened…'

'How?' he burst out. 'Mama, I don't even know whether I can. This is the first time I've ever felt it was possible, but now…not only do I feel like I don't know her, but, like Elise, I'm not even sure that I can trust her. You're special. Tina was special. But that's all. I can't face what I felt when Tina died—or when I found out Elise was two-timing me. I travel the world. I don't want some woman…'

'Some woman… Does this woman have a name?'

'Sophie.'

'I'd call her Sophie, then,' his mother said calmly. 'or you risk being slapped again.'

'She wouldn't.'

'Why not?'

'It's finished. Over.'

'So you've finished the affair?' his mother enquired calmly, watching her son's face. 'And come back to your mother for Christmas?'

'Yes, but…'

'So why are you saying you'd make a hell of a husband?' Marie said softly. 'If it's finished?'

'I don't… I can't…'

'Does Sophie live at Marlin Bluff?'

'For now, but…'

'You know, I believe I may come to Marlin Bluff for the Millennium celebrations.' His mother's eyes twinkled suddenly, and the likeness to her son was very strong. 'I was thinking of it, and now I'm sure.'

'Mama, don't you dare interfere.'

'Interfere?' Marie threw up her hands in mock horror. 'Of course I won't interfere. Would I ever?'

'It's nothing. I shouldn't have told you.'

'Is it nothing because you don't want to be tied down? Or is it that you don't want to be hurt again?'

Bryn gave an angry shrug. 'I don't know.'

'Well, both reasons are nonsense,' Marie said calmly. 'My son mustn't lack courage—and tell me this: if your Sophie isn't at Marlin Bluff when you return, how will you feel?'

'She'll be there.'

'But if she's not? If she's left, or if she's in the arms of another lover? Another man? What then, my son?'

There was only one answer to that. 'I'd kill him.' The words came out before he even knew they were in his head, and his mother laughed out loud.

'Then I think you'd best go back to Australia via Paris,' she told him, 'and buy this Sophie a Millennium present. A golden ring with a very large diamond springs to mind as being entirely suitable.'

'Mama, don't!' He spread his hands helplessly before him. 'Hell, Mama, how could I make her happy as a husband? Dear God, part of my ability to love died when Tina died, and Elise killed that ability completely. I can't get that willingness to love back. I can't trust. I thought I could, but then Sophie betrayed me and it all came flooding back—how I'd felt then. Now…I don't even know for sure that she loves me, and I don't know whether I have the courage to let myself love her. In fact, I'm almost sure I don't.'

'Then wait a little, stand by and watch her fall in love with another,' his mother said calmly. 'If you can. See how you like that. The alternative is to learn how to commit yourself to loving. My son, you have a little growing up to do, and I think maybe this Sophie is just to the girl to see you do it.'

Sophie wasn't helping anyone to grow up at that moment. She was feeling as if she needed to do some growing up herself.

I'm like a lovesick teenager, she told herself crossly for the hundredth time. She shouldn't care that Bryn was due back at the resort at any minute—that he could walk through the door...

But she did, and it was all she could think of.

The Millennium was so close now. It was December the twenty-seventh; the world was counting down and the prep-arations at the resort had reached frenzy pace. Ellie was coming out to Marlin Bluff every day, the tiny church gleamed as it had never gleamed in its life before, and there were painters and polishers and gardeners, with Ellie and John supervising like two contented mother hens.

The world seemed deliriously happy—so why wasn't she?

December the twenty eighth came and there was still no sign of Bryn. Claire came in to make the final arrangements for her flowers and Sophie welcomed the company. At least when she was working she couldn't go quietly crazy think-ing about the man.

She'd decided on simplicity for Claire's bouquet. Claire volunteered little input into decisions, and Colin, having ensured his wife-to-be was wearing a dress of truly grand proportions, and knowing how much fuss was now being made over the wedding, was content to let Sophie choose.

'Then it's white gerberas, apricot spray roses, white Singapore orchids, misty white statice and fine asparagus fern,' she told Claire, putting a small collection of the chosen flowers together as she spoke. 'Look, Claire. It should tone down the gilt in your dress and make you look…'

'Pretty,' Claire said, and her voice was suddenly wistful. She put out her fingers and touched the fern fronds. 'It's so pretty… Not like my dress.'

'Your dress is beautiful.'

'It's not me.'

'Claire, you'll look lovely.'

'Will I?' Claire shrugged. 'I guess—as long as Colin thinks so.'

'I'm sure he will,' Sophie said warmly, but inside she wondered whether Colin would even notice his bride. He was getting everything that he wanted from this wedding, and Claire was his means of getting it. But…after the ceremony?

'You're not having second thoughts, are you, Claire?' she asked. What a question! Bryn would kill her if he heard, and so would Ellie, but Claire's face was pale and there was no hint of bridal radiance.

'Oh, no. I'm not. How could I?'

'You love Colin?'

'Of course.' Claire twisted her fingers, and Sophie wondered just what had happened to the bubbly Claire she remembered from schooldays. 'Colin makes me feel…I don't know…safe. He tells me what to do. I guess he makes me feel like my world is ordered.'

'You like that in a man?'

'I suppose I must.' Claire managed a smile. 'My dad's always bossy when he's at home.'

'You know, it doesn't hurt to be a bit assertive,' Sophie said softly. 'There's two people in every marriage, and two opinions. If you work on it, maybe Colin could be a friend as well as a husband.'

'Oh, no. Not... I mean... Colin treats me like...like a wife. He never talks to me like a friend—not like Joe does.'

'You and Joe are friends?'

'We are now.' Claire managed a smile. 'I'm so full of pre-wedding nerves that his friendship's the only thing keeping me sane.'

'I see.' Sophie sighed. She did see, only too clearly, but there was no way she could make Claire do the same. So...back to work... 'Okay, then, Claire, let's make a decision on the table arrangements.'

'Shouldn't table arrangements have been organised before this?' The voice from the door made both girls start, and Sophie's heart missed a beat. Bryn... She spun around to face him and felt all the colour drain from her face.

'W...welcome back.'

'Thank you.' There was a brief smile to Claire, but none to her. 'I thought the flowers would be settled by now.'

'They almost are,' Sophie told him, and only she knew just how hard it was to get her voice to work. 'I just need to make final arrangements with Claire.'

'Didn't you order before this?'

'I have ordered.' Damn him, if he could be businesslike, so could she. 'Every flower known to man is coming into the resort in the next couple of days. What I don't need for the wedding I'll be using elsewhere. This resort is awash with flowers...'

'Fine, then.' His face showed no emotion whatsoever. He gave a brief, tight nod and turned away.

'Goodness,' Claire said, frowning. 'He seems...different. Last time I met him he seemed really friendly.'

'He's probably jet lagged,' Sophie said lamely. 'He's just flown in from France.'

'But...'

'He'll be fine, Claire,' Sophie said, summoning strength. He might—but would she? 'Don't take it personally. Okay, let's get on and make these decisions.'

Don't take it personally? How else could she take it?

His face stayed with her for the rest of the day, cold, hard and formal. Was it just jet lag? Or was it that he'd got what he wanted from her and now there was no need to be friendly. She'd tried to betray him, and now she was paying the price.

She made him feel weird!

Bryn lay awake that night, with his dogs once again in his bed, and swore into the dark. What had he expected? He'd hoped against hope that when he saw Sophie again the confusion would be lifted and he would be able to look at her just as he looked at other women—but he couldn't. He'd opened the workshop door and seen her, and she'd been just as lovely as ever...just as desirable...standing there in her overall clutching a roughly made bouquet...

She was gorgeous! The sight of her had almost overwhelmed him, and he'd been curt to the point of rudeness because of it.

Sophie... He stirred uneasily, and his loins started to ache all of their own accord. Dear God, all he had to do was think about her... All he wanted to do was walk across to the chapel, lift her from her own bed and carry her here—by force if necessary—and close the door to stay with her for ever.

For ever?

That was the rub. For ever scared him stupid. If he did say for ever, and then if she sprang another surprise on

him… Another betrayal… He and Tina had been so close—
a pigeon pair who had shared their lives. The death of his
twin had shaken him to the core, and since then his only
foray into commitment had been a disaster. To learn to
share himself again…

He didn't know her, he told himself harshly. How on
earth could he think of marrying her? He hardly knew her!

But…not to marry her?

In the resort safe lay one diamond solitaire. Bryn had
visited a jeweller in Paris and chosen it, but when he'd
arrived back at Marlin Bluff he'd put it firmly in the safe
and left it there.

'I shouldn't have bought it,' he told the dogs. For some
reason Joe was preoccupied and grim these days, spending
little of his spare time at the resort, and Marty and Goggle
were pleased to see their master—and even more pleased
to share his bed. 'It was a crazy idea,' he said now, and
Goggle stirred his stump and rolled over.

'You don't think so?' Bryn demanded. 'Maybe you're
right. Maybe it was a good investment. It'll accumulate in
value and make an inheritance for my grandchildren.'

What grandchildren?

Bryn groaned, rolled over and searched for the oblivion
of sleep. He grabbed his dogs and hugged them close, and
they wuffled dog comfort.

It didn't help.

What grandchildren?

'Sophie?' Rick's voice on the other end of the line sounded
anxious.

'What's wrong?' It was three in the morning Australian
time, and Sophie had flown out of bed to reach the phone.
John had stayed up late—way past his usual bedtime—
talking to Claire; when Sophie had gone to bed they'd still

been talking, so Sophie didn't want him woken now. She stood in the hallway and wondered about the urgency in Rick's voice.

'I'm just checking,' he told her anxiously. 'Sophie, you *are* coming home on the fifth?'

'Of course I'm coming,' she told him. 'Why would I change my mind?'

'It's just…the word's gone around florist circles that Bryn Jasper's playing games.'

'What do you mean?'

'Sophie, Jasper was desperate to get another florist and you were a godsend.'

'I know that.'

'And you quit?'

'Yeah, but…'

'One of my clients's a gossip columnist, flying out for the celebrations, and she was talking to me about it this afternoon. The Millennium's huge publicity for Jasper, Sophie. Everyone knows he really needs a florist, and rumour is that he bought the chapel to keep you happy.'

'But he wants the chapel,' she said slowly. 'I don't see the problem. He wants to restore it…'

'Don't you believe it.' Rick's voice sounded worried. 'According to my source, he only wants the land. This woman says he's a ruthless businessman. He'll get what he wants from you and then do what he wants with the chapel. Has he made any legal promises?'

'No, but…'

'He'll want that wedding in the resort, Sophie,' Rick warned. 'Whatever he's told you, he wants the resort on the map, not your grandfather's chapel. He'll keep you happy until the last minute but then…' Rick hesitated and she heard personal worry kick in—the real reason he was ringing. 'Whatever…if Bryn kicks your grandfather out of the chapel on the day of the Millennium…you'll still come back by the fifth?' His voice grew wheedling. 'There's five huge functions booked for January and I need you. Hell, Sophie…'

'I'll be back,' Sophie said automatically. 'Rick, this is nonsense. I trust Bryn.'

'Do you, dear?' he asked. 'Well, that's fine, but if I were you… The man's a ruthless businessman, Sophie. Ask yourself how safe verbal promises really are.'

Verbal promises were as safe as houses.

Sophie went back to bed, but there was no way she could sleep. Rick's call had unsettled her too much.

Of course they were safe, she told herself. Bryn would never kick Grandpa out and bulldoze the chapel.

But the look on Bryn's face as she'd last seen him washed into her consciousness and stayed. His face harsh and cold. Pleasantry was over—there was only business.

He couldn't do it. To waste all this work…

Her heart told her Rick was wrong, but her head whispered all sorts of insidious nightmares.

Bryn had heaps of money, and the publicity for the Millennium would earn him more. On the other hand, having no superb flowers for his celebrations would be a disaster. Photographers from all over the world would be looking down their noses at second-rate standards.

Bad publicity was worse than no publicity, so…he'd pay a lot to keep her working until the last minute.

No! That was crazy suspicion talking—Rick's suspicious mind. Bryn wasn't like that.

He couldn't be.

Sophie couldn't afford to let Rick's hints affect her. In no time it was December the thirty-first, the last day of the century, and she had to sweat blood if she wanted everything ready on time. She and Louise were up to their arm-pits in flowers and she didn't walk anywhere the whole day. She ran.

So did the entire resort staff. There was no sign of Bryn, but that wasn't surprising. On her brief forays out of her workshop, she recognised the rich and famous, and pho-tographers and journalists from all over the world. Anyone who was anyone was gathering here for tonight's celebra-tion and tomorrow morning's wedding, and everyone would be wanting to talk to Bryn.

Would he be moving on to the next woman?

She couldn't think of that. She didn't have time!

By three in the afternoon Sophie and Louise had the flowers under control. The ocean of flowers had become a mere sea as arrangement after arrangement was swooped on by hotel staff and taken off to its nominated position, and Sophie started on the garlands for the chapel service tomorrow…

'Tea, first,' Louise said as she shifted buckets of fran-gipani and groaned under their weight. 'If I don't have a cup of tea soon, I'll die.' Then she paused as Martha Hunter walked into the workshop.

Martha was secretary to Warwick Heston, the resort manager, and she dealt with the minutiae of resort man-agement. Normally Martha was the embodiment of calm efficiency, but now…she looked stricken.

'What's wrong?' Louise demanded, as Sophie turned to stare. 'Martha…?'

'Sophie, I don't know how to tell you.' The middle-aged woman, usually starched, brisk and frighteningly efficient, now looked close to tears. 'Oh, Sophie…'

'Grandpa…' Sophie's face blanched to death-white and she took two faltering steps forward. 'Something's hap-pened…'

'Oh, no.' Martha shook her head, her eyes brimming behind her glasses. 'No, dear, he's fine. At least I think he is. I don't think he knows yet, but I don't know how to tell him…to tell you.'

'Tell me what?'

'Mr Heston said you must be told straight away.' Martha took a deep breath and squared her shoulders.

'The wedding's been moved again,' she faltered. 'It's not in the chapel any more. It's in the resort's wedding centre, and your grandfather's not doing it.'

'Not doing it?'

'No, dear. The celebrant we usually use—Mr Hamilton—has been given the job.'

CHAPTER TWELVE

THAT was practically all Martha knew.

'I'm sorry, but I don't know more,' she told Sophie. 'Mr Heston only just told me, but he said you should know…because you'll need to reorganise the flowers…and tell your grandfather…' Her eyes fell helplessly to the buckets of frangipani around the workshop. 'Oh, dear, I'm so sorry. I know how much it meant to him.'

'Was it Bryn who reorganised this?'

Sophie's voice was dangerously calm. Somewhere in the back of her mind she'd been expecting this. She'd known. Why had she bothered to ask the question? She knew!

Martha spread her hands. 'I don't know. Honestly, Sophie, I don't. All I know is what I've told you.'

She was genuinely upset, and Sophie could get no more out of her. They stood, the three women, staring at each other while the enormity of what was happening sank in.

'I… It should still be okay,' Martha faltered. 'For the photographs and things, I mean. I guess…'

Yes. The wedding could go ahead beautifully now, Sophie thought numbly. She'd done all the planning. Louise had even helped to do the practice bouquet. If Sophie walked away now she could do it on her own. They could cope without her.

Bryn had timed this announcement brilliantly.

'I hate him,' Sophie said softly, through clenched teeth. 'I'll kill him.'

Martha gave a tight, nervous laugh. 'Oh, Sophie… Don't be…'

'Melodramatic? I'm not being melodramatic. I'll...
I'll...' Sophie stopped and looked Martha straight in the
eye. 'Where is he?'

'I don't know.'

'Martha!'

'It's true,' Martha wailed. 'He hasn't been around all
afternoon. Mr Heston's been trying to find him after he got
the message to change the wedding, but he can't. Sophie,
I honestly don't know.'

'I'll find him.' Sophie carefully wiped her wet hands on
her overalls and took a deep breath. 'And when I do...'

She left her sentence unfinished. She just couldn't think
of anything bad enough to fill in the blank.

Martha was right. Bryn wasn't in the resort, or if he was,
then the coward was hiding somewhere—which Sophie
wouldn't put past him.

'Rat!' she said over and over under her breath as she
searched, and sometimes she said it out loud. 'King-sized
weasel. Toad!'

Rick must have been right. Bryn had planned this from
the start! All this, to get himself a florist!

'Where are you, you fink?'

She did a round circuit of his apartment, the wedding
centre, reception rooms and restaurants, but ended up in the
foyer still without finding him. Warwick Heston was standing by the waterfall, speaking to a slim, elegant woman in
her early sixties, but Sophie was past caring who she was
interrupting. 'Warwick, where's Bryn?' she demanded.

'Sophie...' The hotel manager looked harried, Sophie
thought, flustered and upset and unlike his usual urbane
self. 'Sophie, I'm sorry.'

'Where's Bryn?'

'I don't know.' Warwick turned helplessly to his companion. 'Marie, can I introduce you to Sophie Connell, our chief florist? Sophie, this is Marie Jasper, Bryn's mother.'

'Oh, are *you* Bryn's Sophie?' The woman's face lit with interest.

'I'm not Bryn's Sophie,' Sophie said through clenched teeth. 'And I'm not the resort's chief florist. I've just quit. Mrs Jasper, I'm sorry to have to tell you this, but you have a truly appalling son. Warwick, tell me where Bryn is or I'll kill you, too.'

'You intend to kill my son?' Marie said faintly, but there was a decided twinkle behind her eyes. 'Really?'

'If what he's done kills my grandpa, then I swear I will,' Sophie told her, and there was enough seriousness behind her words to make Marie's twinkle fade. She looked a question at Warwick.

'Sophie's a little upset at the moment,' Warwick told Bryn's mother—*understatement of the year!*—and then he added something surprising. 'And maybe she has cause. Sophie, we didn't know about this—none of the staff did. I promise.'

Sophie looked into his concerned face and she believed him. Okay, then. She wouldn't do murder here. So it was only Bryn.

'So how…?'

'There was a message left for me that the wedding was to be changed,' Warwick told her. 'That's all I know. I rang Colin and he confirmed it. Colin said the wedding's to be in the wedding centre with Mr Hamilton doing it. The man was blunt to the point of rudeness and I could get no more out of him. That's it. That's all I know.'

'But Bryn's behind it.'

Warwick shook his head. 'Sophie, I honestly don't know. I've been trying to find him, too, and his mother's here and he's not here to greet her…'

'Well, maybe you could both keep looking,' Sophie said softly—dangerously—and then she paused and closed her eyes. 'Please...if you can...make him change things back again. Because I don't know how I'm going to tell Grandpa. Dear God...'

Her voice broke on a sob and she turned and half ran out of the foyer, leaving Warwick and Marie staring after her.

'But...she really is lovely,' Marie whispered, almost to herself, and then she turned to Warwick. 'And my son...? I don't understand. There is something so badly wrong here? He really has hurt her?'

'I thought I was a ruthless businessman,' Warwick said, watching Sophie go. 'But if Bryn's behind this...' Warwick shook his head. 'Well, there's more of the Marlin Bluff community left than he thinks. Your Bryn might well have a full-scale mutiny on his hands.'

So where was he?

Once outside, Sophie stopped, at a loss. She'd run out of places to look.

Joe might know. There was a gardener—Hector—watering the potted palms lining the resort steps. On impulse Sophie interrupted him, but instead of directions to Joe, she got worry.

'I don't know where Joe is,' Hector told her. 'And if we can't find him soon we're in trouble. There's so much organisation to be done and he's not here to give orders.'

'Not here...'

'He got a phone call about lunchtime and he disappeared. He hasn't been back since and there's about ten people looking for him.'

'Like Bryn?'

Hector pushed his cap back on his head. 'Mr Jasper? No, we're not looking for him.'

'I can't find Mr Jasper, either.'

'Well, I can tell you where he is.'

Sophie held her breath. 'Where?'

'He's doing my job. I was supposed to be taking the boat out to check the stinger net all the way around. It's a cow of a job—takes about four hours to do a thorough check— but it has to be done. I was just getting in the boat when Mr Jasper came down to the beach with those two damned dogs and said he'd take over.'

'He took the dogs out in the boat…?'

'Oh, they'll be fine,' the man told her. 'They go out with Joe all the time and love it, and since Mr Jasper's been back he's almost taken them over. But I don't know why the boss wanted to go.' He looked at his watch. 'He's been out for two hours now, so I reckon it'll take him another two before he's back. I just hope Joe's back by the time he is. I don't want him getting into trouble…'

What should she do now? Sophie walked slowly down the track, thinking hard. If she couldn't see Bryn for another two hours then she needed to talk to Grandpa. It wasn't fair for Ellie and Grandpa to keep working on the chapel— but she desperately didn't want to tell them what was happening.

Sophie thought of the joy in the little house as she'd left that morning. Ellie and James and the children were working their fingers to the bone to have the place perfect for tomorrow's ceremony, and they'd worked so hard… There were so many dreams about to be shattered.

'He's gone out in the boat to get away from me,' she muttered. 'Of all the cowardly acts! I can't tell Grandpa…' So what else could she do?

It wasn't right that she should break the news to her grandfather before she'd had this out with Bryn, she thought. Maybe there was time to make him see…make him change his mind…

Fat chance!

But…once she'd thought she knew him—she'd thought she loved him! So maybe…

Maybe not. But she could only try. She was desperate enough to try anything.

She turned and walked down to the beach.

Bryn was out there. Sophie could see his boat, right at the back of the netted area. The resort netted a vast expanse, roughly about five acres of sea surface north of the headland. The net stopped sharks—a rarity in these waters—or the more deadly box jellyfish which came in during summer months. Once every couple of weeks scuba divers checked the full length to make sure it hadn't been holed.

As well as that, someone had to do what Bryn was doing—check the top of the net was intact and stretching above the waterline. That kept out the bluebottles—tiny, jellyfish-like creatures which floated on the surface of the water and gave a nasty sting when they came into contact with human skin.

She stood on the beach and watched. His two dogs were in the boat, and from where she stood they seemed peaceful. A man and his dogs, doing a necessary chore—uncaring of the hurt that lay back on the beach.

Damn him. Damn him. Damn him!

It was four o'clock and the beach was close to deserted. Most of the resort guests were starting to wander back to their rooms to ready themselves for the night's activities. Steve, the water sports director, was hauling a couple of rubber dinghies from the water, including the one with the outboard motor that he used for rescue work. On impulse, she ran down to the water's edge.

'Leave it in, Steve,' she told him. 'I need to use it.'

'Why?' Steve frowned at her. 'It's not a recreational boat, Sophie.'

'I need to take it out. Steve, I need to talk to Bryn.'

He frowned again, looking doubtfully out to sea, where his boss steadily checked his nets, then hesitated and finally shook his head. 'I don't know whether Bryn wants to talk to you, Sophie,' he told her. 'I can't think why the hell he wants to check nets, unless it's to get away from people, and he was bloody testy when he left. If I were you, I'd leave him alone. You'll get your head snapped off if you go out.'

'So will he,' Sophie said tightly. 'I know what I'm doing, Steve.'

'Well…'

'Hey, the worst he can do is sack me,' Sophie said, making her voice as light as she could. 'And I'm not afraid of that for a minute.'

How could she be? Not when the last thing she ever intended was to work again for Bryn Jasper.

The dogs saw her first. Bryn was a million miles away. He'd been checking the nets on automatic pilot, and the rest of his brain was hardly functioning. Since he'd returned to Australia he'd been working like a madman, but when he fell into bed at night sleep didn't come.

He was so confused he could hardly think. Damn. Why couldn't he get this sorted in his head? Sophie was only a woman, after all.

If he didn't get her out of his system soon he'd go mad, he told himself over and over. He'd get this Millennium wedding over and then he'd head back overseas, he decided, and he'd stay there.

Warwick could manage fine—in fact, Warwick and his staff were so efficient they hardly needed Bryn, even for this Millennium celebration. As it was, Bryn was driving himself into the ground, and Warwick had been looking at him strangely because of it. In the past, he'd been leaving more and more to his manager, but this week he'd demanded responsibility back again. He needed to be busy or he'd go crazy!

But his head was still falling to pieces. So much so that this afternoon he'd walked down to the beach and demanded to do the most tedious, time-consuming job he could think of—one where there were no people.

And one where there were no flowers! Sophie's flowers lay all around the resort, and he couldn't get away from them. Stylish and beautiful and... Oh, God, stop thinking of Sophie. If only the pain he'd felt when his twin died didn't keep welling back, and the humiliation Elise had left him with... It sat in his heart like a warning...

Then the dogs raised their paws onto the bow and started barking. Bryn shielded his eyes against the sun to see who was coming.

Sophie.

His heart stilled.

He'd hardly seen her since he'd got back to Australia, and that was the way he wanted it, yet here she was, her little putt-putt dinghy motoring straight for him.

She didn't come right up to him. Bryn's boat was wooden-hulled and stable, which was why he could share it with his dogs, and her boat was rubber. She had enough sense to know that if she came near enough for the dogs to launch themselves into her dinghy, their paws would rip holes and she'd go down with her ship—or she'd be forced to submit to being rescued by Bryn, which was the last thing she wanted.

She stopped ten feet away and waited while Bryn tried to silence his dogs, which he did—finally—but only after three minutes of futile threats. Eventually he solved the problem by taking both of their muzzles in his hands and holding their jaws closed.

When silence finally reigned, Bryn's patience was at an end, and he had none to spare for Sophie.

'What do you want?' he asked coldly.

As a beginning it was hardly promising. Bryn's words were intended to drive her right back into shore again, which was what he wanted—wasn't it? He didn't have a clue how to handle himself here. It was as if his back was up against some invisible wall, and he wasn't sure what he was fighting—or why.

'I want to speak to you,' Sophie said menacingly. 'Now.'

'Surely whatever you need to say to me can wait until I get back to shore.'

'No. I'll be gone by then.'

'What do you mean?' He stared. 'What do you mean— *gone*?' Why was his world suddenly standing still? he thought blankly as he heard that the one harsh word. *Gone...*

'I mean I'm leaving your resort and I'm never coming back,' Sophie told him. 'I've been searching my brain, but there's nothing more I can do to fight you. You've won, Bryn Jasper. You've won your damned wedding, you've won your flowers, you've won everything you planned to win, and you don't give a damn about how many little people you hurt in the process. You've manipulated and you've deceived and you've cheated, and if I never see you again in my life it'll be too soon. That's all I wanted to say to you.'

Before he could say a word—before he could even re-act—she put her motor back into gear and turned for shore. He was left holding his dogs and staring after her in stunned amazement.

Bryn stayed stock still, stunned, for a whole ten seconds. What had she said? What on earth was going on? With an oath, he released his dogs and gunned his own motor into action.

The dogs started barking again. They'd been bored stu-pid checking nets and this was much more fun!

Sophie's motor was a ten-horsepower tiddler. His was a two-hundred-horsepower workhorse. Even with her head start, there was no way she could outpace him. In a minute he was pushing past her boat and cutting across her bow, forcing her to veer sideways.

'Stop!' he yelled over the motor noise, and over the noise of the dogs. 'Sophie, stop!'

She hardly heard. There were tears of anger and morti-fication streaming down her face, she could hardly see, but she veered to the right around him and kept on going. Bryn swore, and outgunned her again.

'Sophie, stop!'

'No! Go away…' It was a whisper which Bryn couldn't hear, but he could see her face—and he could see her dis-tress.

Suddenly that was all that mattered. His own reluc-tance—his own concerns—fell away. Sophie was in trou-ble. Her face was tear-streaked and pale and there was real distress in her voice. What the hell…?

This was useless. She could go on veering around him all afternoon, and he needed to be near her. He needed to know…

So he turned again to match Sophie's direction, but this time he didn't try to move across her bow. He simply ran his boat alongside hers, tugging the dogs back from the side of the boat as he did, so they couldn't launch themselves at her, and shoving their backsides down onto the floorboards with sheer force.

He couldn't talk to Sophie with the dogs barking like this, and he couldn't do anything at all if he was holding their muzzles. So...

'Sit!' he roared, with all the authority at his command. 'Stay!' To his amazement, they did.

Then, ignoring the desperate look on Sophie's face—he could think about that when he was close to her—he drew his boat closer...closer...until he could put out his hand and grab the hand-rope running along the rubber side of her dinghy.

The dogs wouldn't stay where they were for ever. Already they were starting to rise, and they'd launch themselves at her and have Sophie sunk if he didn't move fast. 'Sit!' he yelled again. He gunned his boat until his faster speed and the hold he had on Sophie's boat was pulling them all along.

Then, in two swift, synchronised actions, he cut his motor dead and threw himself over the side of the boat—straight into the dinghy to land at Sophie's feet. The dinghy motored on, with two people aboard, and the boat containing the two dogs was left to drift aimlessly wherever it liked within the confines of the nets.

The dogs stared out of their boat with stunned dismay and started barking hysterically, but the gap between the boats was already too big for them to jump. They stared and barked and jumped about the boat, but they didn't jump overboard. They might be dopey but they weren't totally stupid!

Which left Sophie in her dinghy with the man she hated most in the world lying right at her feet. 'Get...get out.'

She was so angry she could hardly make her voice work. 'Get out!'

'No.' Bryn got to his knees, leaned forward and switched off her motor, which left two little boats now floating adrift. On the beach, Steve watched their antics with stunned amazement. What the hell...? He reached for his binoculars, but Bryn and Sophie were far too preoccupied to notice.

'Sophie...' Bryn's voice was so low even she could hardly hear it. He was watching her face and his eyes were filled with concern. The harsh rejection he'd shown her five minutes ago had gone completely. 'Sophie, what is it?'

'Go away.' Sophie's tone was almost hysterical. 'How can you ask?'

They'd floated close to the net, and seaweed had caught on the outer edge. She looked frantically around for a weapon—some way to drive him away—and there was only that. She hauled it out of the water and threw it at him—a great sodden mass.

It was futile—a crazy, childlike gesture, and as stupid as throwing jellyfish at him—but it was all she could think of. There was nothing she could do to fight him.

'You...' She broke off in a sob, but then, instead of going away, Bryn gathered her in his arms and held her, seaweed and all.

'Sophie, tell me...'

She held herself rigid in his grasp, silent sobs racking her body. The seaweed dripped steadily between them, soaking them both. 'How dare you...? Let me go...'

'Not until you tell me what's wrong.'

As if he didn't know! Sophie gave an angry gasp. 'What's wrong? *What's wrong?*' It was *so* hard to get her voice to work when he was holding her! She hauled away from him and managed a glare. 'You know. Don't pretend,' she managed. 'I was crazy to trust you. Rick told me you'd just promised us the wedding to get yourself a decent florist, and he said you'd go back on your promise the minute you didn't need me. I didn't believe him. Stupid me. I was naive…'

She broke off and buried her face in her hands. 'I can't believe you did it to me,' she whispered. 'I can't believe you did it to Grandpa.'

Bryn stared down at her for a long moment, then pulled her hands down. The dogs' barking was growing fainter as they drifted further away, but Bryn wasn't thinking of them. This was his Sophie, in more trouble than he'd ever seen her. *His* Sophie!

He forced her face up to meet his.

'I haven't broken any promise,' he said steadily. 'Sophie, I don't understand what the hell this is all about, but I swear I've broken no promise.'

'You made Colin change his mind again.'

'I made Colin…' Bryn stared, his brain working overtime. 'You mean Colin's cancelled the wedding?'

'No.' Sophie choked on a sob. 'Of course he hasn't, because that wouldn't work for you, would it, Bryn Jasper? As if you don't know what he's done… He's just rescheduled it. He's made a last-minute alteration to our plans—or rather, to Grandpa's plans—when it's too late for me to withhold my services. The flowers are done, the wedding goes ahead—but in the resort and with a marriage celebrant.'

'But…' Bryn took a deep breath. He stared down at her pale face, and there was appalled comprehension in his eyes. 'You're kidding,' he said faintly.

'But you knew!' She threw the words at him like a taunt. 'You knew Grandpa wouldn't get his wedding.'

'Sophie, I didn't.'

The words were flat, harsh and final. Bryn swore again, very softly, and he pulled Sophie in to lie against him—whether she willed it or not. 'Sophie, I swear I didn't,' he told her. 'I swear this has nothing to do with me. I would never hurt you.'

'But…you have,' she whispered against his chest. Oh, God, he felt so good—so right. How could her heart betray her like this? To fall for such a man… 'You have hurt me. You don't want me. You made love to me but it was all…all just to get what you wanted. You don't want me now.'

This was the time for him to agree, he told himself helplessly—to say that what was between them had just been a brief affair. He could still walk away.

No. Not while she lay against him—while his face was in her hair and she felt like a part of him…

'Bryn…why did you make love to me?'

'Why…'

There was no answer to that but the truth, and suddenly the truth was no longer fearful. He could put the pain of Tina's death and Elise's betrayal in the past and find the courage to love. To take this woman as his own…

As for his fear of commitment; commitment was already made. He couldn't bear to let her go. Not now. Not ever. She was his Sophie—his love. He put her at arm's length, looked into her tear-drenched eyes and his heart melted within him.

'Sophie, I made love to you because I wanted to,' he said, and his voice was steady and sure. Deep within, there was something happening that was so momentous he could hardly take it in. There was a great, joyous blooming of celebration and love, so great he wanted to shout for joy—or kiss her.

But he had to make her see, to undo the hurt he'd caused. He must...

'You were no one-night stand. I wanted to make love to you more than anything in the world,' he said softly, and his lips moved in her hair. 'Then, when I thought that you'd been using me, I thought it was easier to stay as I was. You see, ten years ago I lost my twin sister, and while I was still grieving I fell in love. That love was stupid. Elise threw it back in my face. Since then I've built a barricade around my emotions to not let myself be open to hurt. But now...'

'Now...?'

'Now it's you who's hurting and I can't bear it. I love you, Sophie,' he said softly. 'With all my heart, I love you. From the first moment I met you I've fought to hide my feelings, and I've been stupid. I love you, my heart, and I always will, now and for ever—and there's no way I could betray you or hurt your grandfather. I don't know what's going on with the Millennium wedding, and I'll try to change things back again, but if I can't... Your hurt is my hurt, Sophie, and I'll share it. I'll take as much of it onto myself as you'll let me.'

The seaweed dripped steadily between them but neither noticed. There was only each other—and the truth.

Sophie stared, wondering, up into Bryn's face. He met her gaze with solid, loving calm and Sophie knew beyond doubt that what she saw was the immutable truth. What she saw was love. She closed her eyes and tears started sliding down her face again.

'Sophie...' He swore and hauled her into him again, so that her tears were soaking into his shirt. 'Damn, Sophie, don't cry. I swear this wedding...the change...has nothing to do with me. Don't cry...'

'Don't stop me.' Somehow she managed to get the words

out, though she sounded half drowned. 'I don't cry. I never cry. Before I met you I hadn't cried for years. But, Bryn, don't stop me now.'

'Why not?' He kissed the top of her curls. 'Why not, my Sophie? You must believe me.'

'I do believe you,' she whispered. 'Oh, Bryn, I do. But I always cry when I'm as happy as this.'

'Always?'

'Always…' She hiccupped, and then raised her face to be kissed. 'I've just never been this happy before, or this much in love—so you'd better get used to it.'

There were a few matters that needed immediate attention.

Firstly, there were the dogs.

When Sophie and Bryn finally surfaced, the dogs' boat had drifted towards the shallows; they were barking at the back of the waves and were almost hoarse. Their master and Sophie were doing really interesting things in the dinghy, and there was no way they could join in!

Steve had decided to wade out to fetch the dogs when they finally came to their senses enough to motor to shore.

'Sorry, Steve,' Bryn said, as they hauled the dinghy up the beach. The dogs launched themselves with slavish adoration at both of them. Bryn held Sophie so tight that they didn't fall over, and the dogs soon took themselves off to chase seabirds.

'If I may say so…' Steve's grin practically split his face. 'You don't look sorry.' He motioned to his lifesaver's binoculars. 'In fact, neither of you have looked the least bit sorry for the last twenty minutes.'

'Yeah, right!' Bryn grinned and held Sophie tighter. 'Steve, do you want a New Year's bonus in your pay packet?'

'I might.'

'Then babysit a couple of dogs for us,' Bryn told him. 'We have things to do.'

'I'm sure you have.' If it was possible for Steve's grin to widen it did then, and Sophie blushed from the toes up—but Bryn's hand held hers and he gripped her hard.

'Yeah, that too.' His eyes gleamed down at his love, full of the promise of things to come. 'But first there's the small problem of a wedding. We need to see John and find out what the heck is going on.'

'Whose?' Steve yelled as they disappeared up the beach, hand in hand. 'Whose wedding? You keep him honest, Sophie Connell.'

Her blush turned to crimson.

CHAPTER THIRTEEN

EVERYONE seemed to be in John Connell's kitchen.

John was seated at the table, looking grave, Ellie and James and the children were milling around, looking confused and upset, and Bryn's mother and Warwick were by the door, with Warwick looking concerned and Marie looking just plain bewildered.

There was also Louise, standing with Warwick's secretary Martha, and Hector. Even the Labradors, Lily and Matilda, were there, asking for back-rubs from everyone but being totally ignored—because there was also Colin.

Colin had the floor and he was rigid with rage. As Bryn and Sophie walked in, he turned on them with fury.

'Where are they? Where the hell are they?'

'Where the hell are who?' Bryn asked mildly. Bryn had the air of a man who didn't give a damn about the Millennium wedding. The world's photographers and journalists could disappear in a puff of smoke right now and he wouldn't care less. He had what he wanted right here at his side and he needed nothing else.

'Claire,' Colin spat. 'And that man who calls himself a gardener. Scarface.'

'He means Joe,' Hector said mildly. 'I was just getting concerned about him myself, Mr Jasper. That's why I thought I'd come here and ask if anyone had seen him.'

'He's done something with her,' Colin shouted.

'You mean Joe's done something with Claire?' John spoke from where he was sitting at the table, then he looked across at Bryn and Sophie. His gaze intensified, lingering on his granddaughter and the man at her side, and something lit behind his eyes.

'Well, children,' he said softly. 'Well, well...'

Bryn's arm was still around her waist. She tried to draw away but he'd have none of it, and, from the other side of the room, Marie's eyes also lit with interest. Marie wasn't much interested in Colin, but she was exceedingly interested in her son, and he was holding the woman who'd been threatening to kill him...

But Colin wasn't to be deflected.

'He's taken her. Joe's taken Claire,' Colin was shouting. 'He bloody would. Do you know how much she's got? She's worth a bloody fortune.' He was practically screeching in rage. 'If he gets his hands on her money...'

'I think that's enough,' John said, hauling his attention with reluctance from Bryn and Sophie. He rose, and his quiet presence filled the room. This man could hold a cathedral in thrall. 'Mr Draffus, Claire spent much of last night talking to me, and at the end of it she came to a very solid, very sensible decision. She's decided she doesn't want to marry you. I'm sorry, but there it is. I didn't tell anyone here, because there was always the possibility she'd change her mind, but that's what she was going home to tell you.'

'She did.' Colin was so angry now that he was past caring about what he said. 'Stupid bitch. She rang me this morning and said the whole wedding's off.' He stabbed an accusatory finger at John. 'I knew it was your doing. I knew it. I told her not to be so bloody stupid. Her parents are back in the country now, so I told her father the whole thing was a fiasco and there was no way she was coming near you again. He agreed. And then Scarface arrived...'

'Joe,' John said slowly.

'He came in without as much as a by-your-leave and

stuck his oar in. Said Claire was to do what she wanted and we were to stop bullying her. So then her father told him to get out, but he wouldn't, and I hit him…'

'You hit Joe?'

'Not hard enough,' Colin said grimly. 'Claire was screeching at us and crying but her mother dragged her off to her room, then Daniel and I threw him out and things settled. I rang you then.' Colin turned and stabbed a finger at Warwick. 'I got the receptionist and left a message saying we'd still be getting married, only we weren't coming near the old man again. We'd use the resort's wedding centre and the wedding celebrant we booked in the first place. This preacher wasn't getting near Claire again. So her mother went up to tell Claire to pull herself together—the wedding was going ahead.'

'And Claire agreed?' It was Bryn. The smile had died completely from his voice. This man was a bully, and there was no room for laughter here.

'She was gone. She must have legged it out the window. I knew she'd come here, to cry on the old man's shoulder, so I came here, and then I found out your bloody gardener's missing…'

'Colin came here and started abusing Grandpa,' Ellie told Sophie, speaking across Colin's fury. 'So I rang Warwick to find out what was going on. Warwick said he'd come straight here to try and sort it out, and then, just as Warwick and Martha and Louise and…Marie, is it?…' Ellie was obviously trying to sort people out as she spoke. 'Just as Marie arrived, Hector came here looking for Joe. When Colin knew Joe had disappeared, he went ballistic.'

'He's soft on her,' the man shouted. 'That's where she'll be. He's been hanging around her for weeks.'

'He loves her,' Sophie said softly from the safe circle of

Bryn's arm, and suddenly everyone in the room was look-ing at her.

'He... Joe loves Claire?' Bryn looked down at Sophie and his eyes furrowed. 'I don't understand.'

'Joe loves Claire but he doesn't think he's good enough for her,' she said softly. 'But if Colin and her father have been bullying her, and if Colin hit Joe...' She smiled, a tiny, tremulous smile that showed the dawning of happi-ness. 'Oh, if they've found the courage...'

The phone rang. They all stood, staring down at the in-strument on the kitchen bench, as if it could impart infor-mation just by ringing. John finally lifted it. He spoke briefly and then he listened—and smiled. He turned away and spoke softly into the receiver, and he replaced it onto the handset as if he was blessing a child.

'That was Joe and Claire,' he said softly—peacefully. 'They're ringing from Cairns. They've just rung Claire's parents to tell them one wedding's off and another's on, so could I please put it in my diary a month from today— that's the first day they can do it legally. And, Bryn, Joe sent you his apologies but he's taking today off. They'll come back for the Millennium celebrations, but today they thought they'd go shopping for a ring and then take Claire's yacht out and enjoy themselves. He hopes you understand, but even if you don't, that's what's happening.'

John chuckled, the deep, robust chuckle of a man su-premely pleased with what he'd achieved, and then, slowly, every face in the room turned to look at Colin.

'A month...' Colin's face was practically puce. 'Mar-ried? They can't...'

'Claire said to tell us all she was very sorry for the trou-ble she's caused,' John said mildly. 'But I told her no Millennium celebration was worth a lifetime of regret, and she's agreed. Oh, and Joe said thanks very much for hitting him, Colin. For some reason he thinks it's the best thing you've ever done—it gave Claire the courage to be herself.'

There was fascinated, awed silence. This, then, was final, and finally Colin realised it. He swore, and swore again.

'But...they're taking the yacht out—and I don't even own it,' he whispered, appalled realisation dawning. 'My mates are all expecting a holiday on it, and I said I'd use Claire's money to fix Ted's airfare...'

His face whitened and he stared around, as if expecting sympathy, but there was no sympathy here. There was nothing more to be said—and Colin turned on his heels and walked from the room.

'There is the little matter of what we tell the press,'

It was Warwick, getting back to business two minutes later when the exclamations were easing. It was hard to be upset with this outcome, but...

'Tell them what?' Ellie asked. And then her hands flew to her face. 'Oh, no! Of course. Now we don't have a Millennium wedding. Unless Claire and Joe... Oh, Grandpa...'

'We don't need a Millennium wedding,' John said strongly—sternly. 'Even if I could do it legally, there's no way I'm pressuring that young couple. They need time to get to know each other. Too much has happened too fast.'

'But the press...' Warwick was almost recovered from the shock and his mind was working fast. 'Good grief, Bryn, what do we tell them? To bring them from the other side of the world on false pretences...'

'And all the wedding flowers,' Louise wailed, realisation dawning. 'The flowers Sophie and I planned. I wanted to do them so much...'

'Maybe you can still.'

It was Marie, her eyes still resting on Bryn and Sophie—

in fact, throughout Colin's diatribe, her eyes hadn't moved. She didn't know Colin or Joe or Claire. She'd been in Australia for a whole four hours and she was *very* confused.

But she did know her son, and the look on Bryn's face was one she'd thought she'd never see. Marie's twinkle was back with a vengeance, and her son had inherited his lightning-fast planning reflexes from his mother.

'I see no reason why we still shouldn't have a Millennium wedding,' she said happily. 'Isn't it lucky I packed my wedding dress? I just thought I might bring it with me. My dream has always been that my son's bride would wear it, and I believe it may be just the right size!' As the rest of the room turned to stare at her, Marie's twinkle deepened. 'Well, my son?' Her eyes quizzed him with love. 'Well?'

'Well, what?' Ellie stared at Marie, bewildered, and then slowly turned to look at Bryn—and suddenly all the room was looking at the linking of two hands, and at Sophie…

'Mama, we can't do it,' Bryn said, and the words were torn from him with reluctance. His grip on Sophie's hand tightened. 'There's the little matter of a month's notice.'

'But I don't understand,' Ellie wailed. 'I don't understand any of this.'

But then she looked more closely at Sophie's face. Her eyes dropped to Sophie's hand, her fingers entwined in Bryn's, and, as knowledge finally dawned, Ellie let out a whoop that could have been heard all the way to Cairns. 'Oh, no! Oh, yes! Oh, Sophie…'

'What is this—a month's notice?' Marie demanded, not to be deflected from her wonderful idea. 'Bryn, you love your Sophie, yes?'

'Yes, but…'

'And you—Sophie—do you love my son?' Marie directed her gaze straight at Sophie, and there was no room for dissembling.

'Yes,' Sophie said, and the room stilled absolutely. Even Ellie fell silent. Sophie looked up at Bryn and her world steadied. 'I do.'

'But we need a marriage licence.' Bryn's eyes were caressing his love as if it didn't matter. 'It must be processed a month before the wedding.'

More silence, while the assemblage took this in.

It was John who broke the silence. With a smile as broad as his face, he walked around the table and gathered Sophie and Bryn together in an embrace.

'My children. Are you sure?'

'We are.' Bryn tore his eyes from Sophie and met John's gaze, and anyone who read his face could know no doubt. His love and his pride were transparent to all the world. 'Absolutely, sir. If you permit?'

'I permit.' John looked at his beloved granddaughter and he smiled. 'You don't reach my age without knowing true love when you see it. And you, my Sophie? Am I right in believing that you'd marry tomorrow if you could?'

'I'd marry tonight.'

'Then I'll marry you,' John said.

They stared. 'But…' Bryn's voice faltered. 'I don't see how…'

'Your marriage celebrant marries you before the law,' John said simply. 'I marry you before God. The law requires a month's notice, but God is not so rigid. You'll need to sign a legal piece of paper in a month's time, but tomorrow I will marry you before God, and before anyone else you would like to witness your love. Certainly I'll marry you tomorrow. Nothing would give me greater pleasure.'

Bryn stared at John for a long moment, then turned to

Sophie, and the rest of the room might well have not existed.

'What do you say, my Sophie?' he said gently—so tenderly that her breath caught in her throat. 'I'll not have you rushed. The world can go jump as far as I'm concerned. I don't give a damn for the Millennium any more. But if you'd like to marry tomorrow, there's nothing I'd like better. If tomorrow's not too soon…'

Sophie stood with her hands holding Bryn's. She looked up into his eyes and she felt as if her heart should surely burst.

'Bryn, no ceremony could ever be too soon,' she whispered. 'I'm married to you right now, my heart.'

January the first, the year 2000, two a.m., New York time.

The party Rick was attending was going strong and all New York was awake. The whole world was awake, and at two a.m. Rick turned on the television.

'It's the Millennium wedding we've been hearing about,' he explained to Josie. 'Bryn Jasper's show. Sophie's doing the flowers. I need to see…'

Then his jaw dropped almost to the floor, because, instead of an unknown bride, the Millennium bride was none other than Sophie.

For a moment Rick thought he must be seeing things— but it was definitely Sophie. She was wearing an exquisite dress in hand-embroidered silk embossed with silver, soft with age and fitting her lovely figure to perfection. Rick had never seen her look so lovely, and beside her, looking so handsome…

'It's Bryn Jasper,' someone breathed, and the room grew quiet. 'It's Bryn Jasper and Sophie…'

'It must be make-believe,' someone else said. 'Pretend.'

'No.'

Rick said the word out loud, and suddenly every single person in the room agreed with him. This could be no pretence.

The man and the woman standing before the proud old man in the crimson robes radiated their love from half a world away, and the love on their faces shone with a brilliance that none could doubt.

In Marlin Bluff the new Millennium was nearly a day old, and everyone was watching the marriage of two lovers.

The little chapel had doors which folded back, opening this place of worship to the sea. Here, since times long past, man and woman had stood together to become one.

But...this wedding was different.

For a start, this wedding was watched by millions. Television cameramen recorded every moment and sent it beaming around the world for all to see. There were people packed in the little church and standing out on the headland. There were people up in the trees which were garlanded with frangipani. There were flowers and more flowers...

But, in a way, this wedding was exactly the same as all previous weddings. There was one man and one woman. One love.

'Do you take this woman...?'

Bryn looked down at his lovely bride and his heart swelled with pride and with his love. His Sophie. His wife.

'I do.'

'And you, Sophie... Do you take this man...?'

Sophie thought her heart would burst. 'I do.'

There was such joy. All around them were the people they loved. Marie was watching from the front pew, her eyes misting with tears, memories of another bride in just this dress mingling with the joy of what was happening now. Love past. Love to come...

Ellie and James were there, their hands entwined, their children at their sides. This wedding stood as a reaffirmation of their love, as it did for millions. Joe and Claire stood radiantly watching. Their turn would come. For Claire, this made things perfect. Even more perfect! There wasn't a dry eye in the church.

This was the Millennium wedding—a wedding which was a gift—a wedding that was different, and yet the same.

For Sophie, there was only Bryn, and for him there was only Sophie, from this day forth...

They stood hand in hand together before the altar and John Connell's words were a blessing all by themselves.

'I now pronounce you man and wife.'

No one who watched this wedding could doubt for one moment that this was a wedding that was blessed. This was one love that would last a lifetime.

Or a Millennium.

The worldwide cameras watched to the last. Joe, kilted in full Highland regalia, piped them from the church, and as Sophie was lifted into her husband's arms and carried to the waiting car, she tossed her bouquet high among the crowd. It landed right where she'd intended—in Claire's outstretched hands.

The cameras recorded the clatter of cans and old shoes until the car rounded the bend, and then they panned to Claire, burying her face in Sophie's fragrant bouquet.

Her nose came out wrinkled. She frowned, and put her fingers down among the flowers.

'Joe,' she said slowly as the sound of his bagpipes died away.

'Yes, love?'

'Why do you think Sophie carried a jellyfish in her bouquet?'

MILLS & BOON®

Makes any time special

Enjoy a romantic novel from
Mills & Boon®

Presents...™   *Enchanted*™   TEMPTATION.

Historical Romance™   ▲ **MEDICAL ROMANCE**®

COMING NEXT MONTH

MILLS & BOON®

Enchanted™

KIDS IS A 4-LETTER WORD by Stephanie Bond

When Jo Montgomery found herself having to take three kids to the most important meeting in her career, she was frantic. Then she met the children's father, gorgeous widower John Sterling, and she knew her troubles had just begun...

MARRIAGE FOR MAGGIE by Trisha David

When Devlin Macafferty and his small son literally crash-land onto Maggie's private island, they're both in need of refuge. And as Devlin soon comes to realise, desperately in need of a woman like Maggie too...

THE BABY PLAN by Liz Fielding

Amanda's biological clock was ticking away furiously— and when she met gorgeous Daniel Redford, she began to fantasise about him as the father of her baby. Determinedly, she set her plan in motion. But she hadn't counted on falling in love...

THE BRIDAL SWAP by Leigh Michaels

Had Jax Montgomery's fiancée got cold feet—or was Jax having second thoughts? Either way he needed a replacement bride—and was most insistent that, since he'd hired Kara as his wedding organiser, she must be the one to take on the role...

Available from 7th January 2000

*Available at most branches of WH Smith, Tesco, Martins,
Borders, Easons, Volume One/James Thin
and most good paperback bookshops*